"I'm a very hard worker, Mr. da Rocha. Surely you're aware of that?"

"I can see you have excellent references."

"But you're not sure?"

"I'm never sure of anyone," he responded immediately. "My trust is earned."

"Then we're at an impasse," she pointed out, her own expression neutral, green eyes slightly narrowed as she regarded him. "You need cover for Amanda, and I'm the best option you have."

"You're very confident."

"Yes," she said with a shrug, the silk of her blouse rippling over her slender body like a waterfall. For a moment, Salvador's eyes dropped lower, and a little flame of heat flickered in the pit of her stomach. It came without warning and caught Harper by surprise. She tamped down on it immediately, refusing to acknowledge the effect someone like Salvador could have on her. In this moment, she wasn't a woman and he wasn't a man—they would be working together, closely, for many hours a day, and she'd learned the hard way that it was never a good idea to mix business with pleasure.

Clare Connelly was raised in small-town Australia among a family of avid readers. She spent much of her childhood up a tree, Harlequin book in hand. Clare is married to her own real-life hero, and they live in a bungalow near the sea with their two children. She is frequently found staring into space—a surefire sign she is in the world of her characters. She has a penchant for French food and ice-cold champagne, and Harlequin novels continue to be her favorite-ever books. Writing for Harlequin Presents is a long-held dream. Clare can be contacted via clareconnelly.com or on her Facebook page.

Books by Clare Connelly

Harlequin Presents

Crowned for His Desert Twins
Emergency Marriage to the Greek
Pregnant Princess in Manhattan

Passionately Ever After...

Cinderella in the Billionaire's Castle

The Cinderella Sisters

Vows on the Virgin's Terms
Forbidden Nights in Barcelona

The Long-Lost Cortéz Brothers

The Secret She Must Tell the Spaniard
Desert King's Forbidden Temptation

Visit the Author Profile page
at Harlequin.com for more titles.

Clare Connelly

—

THE BOSS'S FORBIDDEN ASSISTANT

PRESENTS

ISBN-13: 978-1-335-59277-4

The Boss's Forbidden Assistant

Copyright © 2023 by Clare Connelly

For questions and comments about the quality of this book,
please contact us at CustomerService@Harlequin.com.

Harlequin Enterprises ULC
22 Adelaide St. West, 41st Floor
Toronto, Ontario M5H 4E3, Canada
www.Harlequin.com

Printed in U.S.A.

Recycling programs
for this product may
not exist in your area.

THE BOSS'S FORBIDDEN ASSISTANT

CHAPTER ONE

'You UNDERSTAND WHAT this job involves?'

Salvador da Rocha was staring at Harper Lawson with obvious scepticism, his golden-brown eyes glinting with something like cynicism. She knew enough about the man to have come here expecting his trademark arrogance to be on display, but this was next level. She fought the temptation to remind him that he was hardly in the best bargaining position, given his hardworking personal assistant, who had already done a full handover with Harper, was taking a well-deserved two weeks off, leaving Harper alone. He needed Harper, but it was evident he didn't *want* to need her.

'Yes, sir.'

He steepled his fingers beneath his chin, eyes boring into hers. To unnerve her? She wondered if she should save him the trouble and tell him there was nothing he could throw at her that would get under her skin. She'd worked for too many jackasses in her time to be bothered by Salvador—even if he happened to be the head of the company and one of the wealthiest men in the world.

'Amanda works long days, sometimes seven days

straight. If I need to travel, she comes with me at a moment's notice. She organises my life. Every part of it. I rely on her completely.'

Harper didn't bat an eyelid—she knew this much from Amanda herself.

'If you accept this job, for the next two weeks you will exist to serve me. Do you understand that?'

She ignored the strange shiver that ran the length of her spine at his choice of words, his accented voice deep and fascinating.

'In exchange,' he continued after a small pause, 'You will be given a sizeable bonus.'

Harper's stomach turned over and her fingertips tingled. A 'sizeable bonus' was exactly why she'd let Amanda talk her into this. As one of her mother's oldest friends, Amanda was one of the few people in Harper's life who understood her personal situation. In fact, it was Amanda who'd pushed Harper to take the job at da Rocha Industries in Chicago two years ago. Because Harper worked hard—harder than almost anyone she knew; she had to. She needed every cent she could earn to pay down her mother's medical costs, and da Rocha Industries was renowned for its generous remuneration packages.

But this 'bonus' was another matter entirely.

'How sizeable?' she asked bullishly. It was a question that might have embarrassed some, but for Harper she'd long passed the point of having the luxury of decorum when it came to money. She had to be mercenary in order to survive. Her skills were many and marketable, and by trading on them she intended to give her mother the very best, most comfortable life she could. Unfortunately, round-the-clock care didn't come cheap.

Salvador's lips flickered with an emotion she couldn't understand, but she tilted her chin defiantly, refusing to be ashamed for asking.

'I think it's a fair question,' she murmured. 'You're asking me to enslave myself to you for a fortnight and, while I'm more than willing to do so, I would like to know what my compensation will be.'

He turned to his laptop and clicked a couple of buttons. 'In addition to your regular salary,' he said, leaving her in no doubt he had her personnel file on screen, 'You will receive four months' pay and the associated benefits.'

'Four months,' she repeated, doing the mental calculations on a small exhalation.

He turned back to Harper and another shiver ran the length of her spine.

'That should give you some insight into the level of service I'll expect.'

She arched her brows. 'I'm a very hard worker, Mr da Rocha. Surely you're aware of that?'

'I can see you have excellent references.'

'But you're not sure?'

'I'm never sure of anyone,' he responded immediately. 'My trust is earned.'

'Then we're at an *impasse*,' she pointed out, her own expression neutral, green eyes slightly narrowed as she regarded him. 'You need cover for Amanda, and I'm the best option you have.'

'You're very confident.'

'Yes,' she said with a shrug, the silk of her blouse rippling over her slender body like a waterfall. For a moment, Salvador's eyes dropped lower, and a little flame of heat flickered in the pit of her stomach. It came without warning and caught Harper by surprise. She tamped it down immediately, refusing to acknowledge the effect someone like Salvador could have on a woman. In this moment, she wasn't a woman and he wasn't a man—they would be working together closely for many hours a day, and she'd learned the hard way that it was never a good idea to mix business with pleasure.

'You understand this is a live-in position?'

For a moment, her eyes flickered beyond Salvador to the view of the lush, tropical rainforest behind him, then to the sparkling South Atlantic that glistened all the way to the white sand beaches of Copacabana, just across the strait.

Ilha do Sonhos, the private island from which the reclusive billionaire lived and worked, was one of the most beautiful places Harper had ever been. As the helicopter had come in over the landing pad, she'd enjoyed the panoramic views of the ocean with the seemingly prehistoric land mass of the island, craggy mountains, rugged cliffs, spiked grasses and enormous, windswept trees creating a lush, green jungle across it. It was wild and almost looked uninhabited, except for this home, all timber and glass, with incredible views in all directions.

'Yes.' She brought her gaze back to his and a jolt travelled through her. She'd seen him from a distance before, at a company event in her native Chicago. He'd spoken only to Amanda and the CFO, Alan Bridges, no one else, but there'd been a magnetism about him. She had found it impossible not to look at him, not to study him. It was his strength and charisma, his confidence and intelligence, the ability he had to walk into a room and command it without even bothering to try. Some people were born with that kind of personality, but not many. Salvador da Rocha was a god amongst men. Working with him, even for two weeks, would be a learning curve she would relish.

'You have an impressive CV,' he said, gesturing to his screen once more.

Damn straight. At twenty-six, Harper had worked for some of the biggest names in the corporate world and, except for that awful business with Peter Cavstock, she had covered herself in glory each and every time. For the last two years, she'd been stationed at the Chicago office of da Rocha Industries, working for the head of North American operations.

'Thank you,' she said with a dip of her head.

'Why did you join da Rocha Industries?' he asked, fixing her with a level stare.

She bit back a desire to ask why it mattered. Wasn't it more important that she did work for him? That she was regarded as indispensable to one of his busiest executives?

'It was an excellent opportunity,' she supplied, the answer revealing very little.

'What do you enjoy about your current role?'

'Enjoyment is beside the point,' she said after a beat. 'It's a job.'

'You don't enjoy what you do?'

'I didn't say that,' she said quietly. 'But I'm not turning up each day looking to be entertained. Whether I enjoy my job or not, I still do it to an excellent standard, always. Every day.'

He pressed his chin to his fingers, steepling them once more. His face was fascinating. She found her eyes clinging to his sharp features longer than was necessary or wise, admiring the chiselled cut of his cheekbones, his jaw, the strength of his patrician nose and the effect his five o'clock shadow had on his overall appearance, giving him a 'devil may care' attitude that was, frankly, quite beautiful. 'Do you like working with Jack?'

She frowned, bringing her errant thoughts back to the present situation. 'Yes,' she said, quickly. 'But I've worked with plenty of people I didn't like. I'm a professional, Mr da Rocha. I come to work to get the job done, and don't leave until I'm finished. Does that satisfy you?'

He studied her for so long, with such intensity, she had a new-found sympathy for bugs under the microscope. Finally, he spoke again, his Brazilian accent every bit as mesmerising as his face.

'Amanda tells me you have some conditions of your own.'

Harper had no doubt Amanda had informed him of those conditions, but Salvador was evaluating her, trying to get a read on her confidence to negotiate for herself.

She fixed him with a direct stare. 'Yes.'

'They are?'

CLARE CONNELLY   13

'I need half an hour a day to myself. During those thirty minutes, I will be completely unavailable.'

Their eyes were locked in a stare that was laced with challenge on both sides. Who would blink first?

'It's an unusual request,' he said.

'To have some time to myself?'

'Such a specific amount of time.'

She compressed her lips, not willing to be drawn on that. 'Mr da Rocha, I have no doubt I can do this job. I would love to work alongside you, and I'm confident I can take care of things in Amanda's absence. I want the money, yes, but more than that, I want the experience. Jobs like this don't come along every day.'

His eyes flashed gold then copper.

'But I will walk away if you don't agree to this condition.'

She'd surprised him. It was evident in the way his mouth stretched, his brows lifting when they met hers.

'I don't like it,' he said after a beat.

She was unflinching, but beneath the desk, away from his view, she kept her fingers crossed. She couldn't budge on this point. Every day, she called her mother in the nursing home and read to her. The doctors weren't sure how much of it her mother understood, but Harper knew it meant the world to her mum, and she had no intention of disappearing into thin air.

'Shall I wait outside while you consider it?' she asked, standing to her full height. She wasn't tall, nor was she short, but she was well aware she had a body that drew the attention of the opposite sex, with curves in what her mother would have called 'all the right places'. It made Harper uncomfortable. While her mother had been adored and feted for her looks, Harper had never welcomed that kind of attention. She pulled her dark-brown hair over one shoulder, then winced, because it was a gesture that spoke of nerves—something she'd trained herself never to show.

His eyes flickered over her body and, despite the fact Harper usually hated it when men looked at her, now the lightest goose bumps lifted her skin, which she preferred to attribute to the sea breeze that brushed in through the ocean-side window, bringing with it a hint of salt in the air.

'That won't be necessary,' he said, finally, echoing her movement and standing, eyes latched to hers so she was overly conscious of the beating of her heart. 'If Amanda put you forward for this role, I'm sure you'll be fine.'

Fine.

Talk about being damned with faint praise, she thought to herself.

Mentally, she came up with a list of substitutions for 'fine'—acceptable, average, bearable, okay—and found that, on further analysis, none of them offered any particularly gratifying appraisal.

'I work long hours,' he explained unnecessarily. 'I will not hesitate to call you when I need something.'

'As you've said,' she agreed with a small nod.

'While you need to be available to me almost the entire day, I expect my privacy to be respected.'

'Don't speak unless spoken to?' she couldn't help responding, with an arched brow and a cynical smile.

'Crude, but accurate.'

Crude or rude, she thought, dipping her head forward to conceal her expression. 'I have no problems with that,' she agreed.

'Then we have a deal, Ms Lawson.'

'Oh, you should call me Harper,' she said, as she moved towards the door. He was right behind her, his stride long, his body so close she could feel warmth emanating off him.

Ridiculous, she chided herself. She wasn't usually prone to that kind of fantasy! He reached past her to open the door, and Harper stepped through it, grateful for some clean air-space.

'We are not friends, Ms Lawson. When these two weeks are over, we will never see one another again. I see no need to refer to you by your first name, nor for you to use mine.'

It was a direct smack-down. A warning: *don't get familiar, don't get comfortable.*

'Very well, Mr da Rocha,' she responded. 'Would you care to point me in the direction of my office?'

Ten minutes later, she was ensconced in a stunning office with panoramic views of the ocean, state-of-the-art computers and screens, and only one small problem: Salvador's office was directly next door, separated by a large glass window, so she could see him, and he could see her, the whole time.

There were blinds, she noted, but only on his side, so he could choose when he wanted to close them or open them, leaving the situation entirely in his hands.

A power dynamic she didn't particularly like, but wasn't willing to challenge—not for the sake of two weeks.

'Amanda has brought you up to speed?'

'Yes, sir.'

'Good. This pile is most urgent. Start on that right away.'

He moved towards the door of her office.

'The chef provides meals at seven in the morning, one in the afternoon, a snack at four and dinner at eight, but naturally the kitchen is stocked and you are welcome to help yourself to anything you require. I eat alone. A room has been made up for you—the housekeeper, Catarina, will take you to it later today. Catarina is your point of contact for anything domestic. Did Amanda leave you with a list of my contacts?'

'Of course.'

'Good.' His frown deepened. 'I don't tolerate mistakes, Ms Lawson. Keep your head in the game and I'm sure the next two weeks will go just fine.'

Adequate, reasonable, acceptable, she thought with a flicker of her lashes.

He left the office, the slight hint of a threat still hanging in the air, so she stared at her computer screen with a sinking feeling in her gut, but only for a moment.

Harper rallied, reminding herself that she wasn't a wallflower; she wasn't someone passive to whom life just happened. She grabbed bulls by their horns to make things work in her favour, and that was exactly what she intended to do right now.

So much depended on the next two weeks. While

her annual salary was excellent, by the time she paid her mortgage and her mother's medical expenses, she wasn't exactly flush. The idea of earning this kind of money, of being able to build a small nest egg just in case, was ultra-appealing.

Maybe even a college fund? a little voice in the back of her mind pushed, but Harper quickly silenced such a silly thought. College had been a pipe dream. One she'd given up on a long time ago. She'd had to, and she hadn't regretted that for a single moment, she reminded herself forcefully. Not when she considered that she'd been able to provide for her mum by going straight out into the workforce.

It wasn't Harper Lawson's fault—none of it was.

Not her fault that, twenty-seven years ago, Amanda Carey had a daughter. Nor that, a year ago, that daughter had become engaged, was getting married in two weeks and 'needed' her mother to be there with her. It was not Harper Lawson's fault that Amanda had taken her first proper leave in eight years, and that Salvador had had to grapple with how he'd come completely to depend on the other woman's calm organisation of his life.

And it was definitely not Harper Lawson's fault that she had eyes the colour of the ocean on a stormy afternoon, eyes the exact same shade as another woman Salvador had once known. Eyes he'd seen fill with delighted excitement and crushing devastation in the course of a few short months. Eyes he'd watch go from sparkling like emeralds to dull like slate over the course of two years. Eyes he would never see again, now that she was gone.

He stood, prowling from behind his desk towards the windows that overlooked the ocean, wishing that he could summon a storm cloud or two to go with his mood.

He didn't like change.

He didn't like people—new people, particularly.

And there was something in Harper Lawson's manner that was particularly unnerving, but he couldn't put his finger on it. Beyond her eyes, there was no other resemblance to Anna-Maria. Anna-Maria had had short blonde hair that hung in soft waves around her face. She'd been tall and statuesque, until chemotherapy had made her so thin he'd thought she might break just by breathing—she very nearly had.

His face tightened into a grimace.

He tried not to think of Anna-Maria, or the baby they'd made and lost, and the way Anna-Maria had given her life for their child, delaying necessary cancer treatment so the baby would have the best chance of living. He tried not to think about the years of friendship with Anna-Maria that had been part of his life— the way they'd played together as children, written to one another as teenagers and then, one drunken night, had taken their relationship to the next level, changing all the parameters of his world.

He tried not to think about any of it, but every now and again it all came back to him, and he almost doubled over from grief. Not just at losing them, but at the fact he hadn't been able to halt death. He hadn't been able to destroy cancer. He'd thrown all his money at it, convinced modern medicine would hold the answer, but he'd been arrogant and stupid.

Their daughter had died, and then Anna-Maria had followed just months later. At twenty-nine, he'd buried his wife, one of his oldest friends. A year later, Salvador was still remembering how to put one foot in front of the other, which made the timing of Amanda's absence even more vexing.

None of this was Harper Lawson's fault, but she was here when he didn't want her to be and, worse, he knew he'd be depending on her just as he had Amanda.

Still, it was only two weeks. He could live with that. In fourteen days, Amanda would be back, Harper would be gone and his life returned to normal, just as he liked it.

CHAPTER TWO

HARPER'S EYES WERE stinging but she had no intention of being the first to leave the office. Not when there was still a mountain of work to do and she was conscious of Salvador just beyond the glass window, working with apparently indefatigable energy, looking as bright and intent as he had when they'd met much earlier that day.

Had it seriously only been today?

She dropped her pen on the desk and leaned back in her chair, surrendering for a moment to a wave of fatigue, closing her eyes and inhaling, letting tiredness wash over as she counted to ten, then opened her eyes and refocused on the screen. The numbers blurred.

She pressed her fingers to her eyes, massaging the lids gently.

'You can go.'

Neither of them had spoken in so long, she'd almost forgotten what he sounded like. But now his voice, accented and fascinating, washed over her from the direction of the door. She swivelled in her chair, heart leaping to her throat. He didn't look *quite* as fresh as the morning, she thought with an instinctive frown.

He'd unbuttoned his shirt at the collar, flicked open to reveal the thick column of his neck, and his sleeves were pushed up to the elbows, showing tanned forearms covered in a light sprinkling of hair. For some reason, the sight of that made her mouth go dry and her tongue feel too thick.

Awareness of him on any level was a disaster.

He was her boss, just as Peter had been. Alarm bells blared; she listened to them.

Swallowing hard, she turned back to her screen. 'I'll leave soon.'

'You're exhausted.' He sounded disappointed, which raised her hackles.

'Well, it's after twelve,' she pointed out, stretching her neck from side to side.

'If this is too much for you…'

She ground her teeth together. 'It's not.' She clicked a few things on her computer then put it into sleep mode. 'Out of interest, what time does Amanda generally work until?' She stood, gathering her things as she spoke.

'Amanda has been doing the job for eight years.'

'I'll take that to mean she usually leaves her desk much earlier.'

'Again, if it's too much for you…'

'That's not what I'm saying,' she repeated firmly. 'But how does that sentence end, anyway? Do you have an alternative to me? Someone else you can fly over to take on this role?'

She was being crotchety but so what? She was tired and he was expecting *way* too much.

She'd clearly hit a nerve, going by the way his brows

knit together and his eyes, so expressive and beautiful, darkened for a moment.

'Did the housekeeper show you to a guest room?'

'I didn't find the housekeeper,' Harper said crisply, resisting the urge to point out that she'd been working all day.

More disapproval. 'Then I'll have to show you.'

'Just tell me where to go and I'm sure I can find it.'

'It's a big house.'

'And I'm a smart woman. Which way?'

He compressed his lips. 'Come on. I will take you.'

Well, this was definitely not going to be a bed of roses for either of them. She told herself he wasn't being antagonistic specifically to her, that he was just an unpleasant, reclusive billionaire, but it was hard not to take it a little personally. She'd worked with some royal pains in the butt in her time, but none quite so outright rude as this guy.

Then again, having a bank balance like his probably eroded the need for civility.

Maybe that was why he had to pay his staff so generously.

She followed him through the house. The panoramic view of the beaches, visible from all windows, was blacked out by night now, revealing the silhouette of ancient trees and sparkly stars in the sky. As they turned a corner, the moon, high and full, cast a silver pathway across the ocean so Harper's breath caught in her throat at the loveliness of it.

Hearing the noise, he turned, frowning, his face a silent question.

'It's so beautiful,' she said, then felt stupid and gauche at such an idealistic comment. But it *was* beautiful.

He didn't respond, which only made her feel worse. Fortunately, their walk was coming to an end. He reached a double set of doors and opened one, pushing it inwards without going inside.

'It's all set up for your stay. There's an office in here too.'

The suite was as luxurious as she'd expect to find in any five-star hotel. She cast her eyes over the large bed, sofa, huge flat-screen TV and French doors, which she presumed led to a balcony.

'Thank you.' Her eyes drifted back to the bed. She couldn't wait to climb into it and find the oblivion of sleep. But first, a hot shower.

She turned back to Salvador, still standing on the other side of the door. She couldn't understand why, but she was glad for it, glad that he was outside, because there was something so masculine about his presence.

'Good night, Ms Lawson.'

He pulled the door closed and she expelled a breath she hadn't realised she'd been holding, glad to be alone, finally, for almost the first time all day. And what a day! Her head was swimming but, damn it, she wasn't just going to meet his expectations, she was going to blow them out of the water. True, the work today had been immense. She'd summarised complex financial reports, responded to myriad emails from all over the world and scheduled a diary that was bursting at the seams. Her head was swimming.

But she'd achieved everything she'd wanted to, and a sense of pride flooded her veins. She concentrated on her breathing, a stillness meditation, as she unbuttoned her blouse and thought hungrily of the shower and that soft-looking queen-size bed.

It wasn't her fault that she'd forgotten her handbag. He'd basically pushed her out of the office in his insistence to show her to her room, but nonetheless he was cursing Ms Lawson as he scooped up the bag and strode through his home with it tucked under his arm.

It's so beautiful.

He recalled her softly voiced admiration at the moon and the beach as he'd come round the corner and the view had hit him square between the eyes. She was right, he grudgingly admitted–, it was beautiful—breath-taking in fact—but it had been a long time since he'd allowed himself to see the view, much less admire it.

At the doors to her room, he knocked twice then waited. Immediately after his second knock, he heard her voice call something, which he took to be an invitation, so pushed the door open, striding in with the intention of placing the bag on the coffee table near the sofa, but he froze two steps into the space.

Ms Lawson was midway through stripping out of her clothes. She'd removed her blouse and pencil skirt but not her silk camisole or lace thong, or, God help him, her heels.

Salvador da Rocha was not a man who was surprised easily but in that moment he lost all command of himself. He could only stare at her, at the curves that had been completely hidden by her outfit, at her creamy soft skin, her delicate breasts and nipples hardened into nubs by the gentle sea air she'd welcomed into the room by throwing open the doors. That same breeze pulled against her camisole now, so it showed the flatness of her stomach, her rounded hips. Her legs were long and curved, perfectly proportioned.

She made a small gasping sound and he lifted his eyes to her face, to lips that were full, pink and parted, her tongue darting out to swipe over her lower lip, her cheeks rosy, her eyes sparkling and filled with electricity. Or was that his blood? Sparks zinged through him and he heard a storm in his ears, in his brain, pushing all thought from his head.

'Mr da Rocha,' she said, but in a strange, strangled voice that showed she was as removed from her senses as he was.

'You…' … *Left your bag,* he finished internally, but he couldn't speak the words, couldn't form them with his tongue. She turned a little away from him, so now the curve of her bottom was visible, and he swallowed a curse because he'd never seen anything quite so perfect as that pert, rounded rear. His hands immediately tingled with the need to feel it fill his palms, to roll his hands over her, to slide his fingers into the elastic of her thong and glide it down her legs until she was naked. He imagined the warmth of her skin, the smoothness, and he groaned, a visceral, aching noise that showed how lost he was.

It had been a long time since he'd been intimate with

a woman. A long time since he'd seen the unclothed form of one.

And now he was staring at his near-naked assistant like some randy schoolboy. It was a sobering thought, pushing his mind back into gear, even when his body was still growing hard, his blood pounding through his veins like a tsunami.

'Why the hell did you tell me to come in?' he demanded angrily.

'I *didn't*!' She gaped. 'You... I...heard a knock...'

'And called out—'

'I squawked,' she said with obvious anger. 'I was in this state!' Her hands gestured unhelpfully to her body, reminding them both that she was undressed. As if he needed the reminder. 'I was trying to say "don't come in".'

'But you didn't say that.'

'No, I was flustered.' Her eyes dropped away, her jaw moving as she ground her teeth together.

He thought back, trying to remember what he'd heard, and realised her story could be plausible. Not in the mood to admit his own mistake, or to apologise, he clung to his irritation like a life raft. 'Well, don't you know how to lock a dammed door?' he muttered, lifting the bag higher. 'You forgot this.'

She recoiled physically, as though he'd slapped her, and he felt instant regret at his angry words. None of this was her fault—not that he'd stalked into her room to find her in a state of undress, or that she was so incredibly, sinfully beautiful. And definitely not that he'd sworn he'd never want another woman. His throat constricted, making breathing difficult, and finally, belatedly, he did what he should have done from the first moment he'd crossed the threshold and seen her like this: he turned his back.

'I didn't think I'd need to lock the door to my own room,' she responded with a voice that was almost ice-like, except for a fine quiver at the end. He suspected he'd done the impossible on day one and upset the assistant Amanda has assured him would be unflappable. Then again, he was pretty sure he was breaking a hell of a lot of HR guidelines right now.

He placed the bag on a table near the door and moved back, spine straight, shoulders tense.

'I thought you called for me to come in,' he said.

'I didn't.' Her cheeks were still flushed, her body on display, he saw, when he chanced a quick glance over his shoulder. The effect was immediate. His cock jerked in his pants and his chest swelled as he inhaled a breath that might as well have been filled with flames for how much it overheated him.

Before Anna-Maria, he'd dated women. He'd slept with women. He'd lived like a normal, red-blooded man with a billion-dollar empire at his fingertips and had had his choice of company any night of the week. He'd made love to women without compunction, without emotion, but Anna-Maria had changed him. Rather, her shock pregnancy had. For the first time in his life, he'd been faced with the consequences of his lifestyle—a careless one-night stand with one of his oldest friends who'd ended up carrying his baby because he'd failed to use a condom. She'd been on the pill, and they'd both been clean, but that hadn't made it okay.

It had also brought him face to face with the ghost of his own past—of his father's neglect and abandonment, of his father's mistreatment of his mother. He'd been reborn that day into a different man. For almost two years, he'd been celibate, the price he considered it his duty to pay, his atonement for what had happened to Anna-Maria, even when he knew he hadn't caused her cancer.

'I had no idea you'd be changing so quickly.' His voice was raspy. God, but she was beautiful. 'You only came back here a few moments ago.'

'Yes, well, it's late and I'm tired,' she snapped, her words husky, almost as though she was close to tears. That had him turning to face her once more, studying her for signs of distress, but she kept her features schooled into a mask of icy disapproval. 'Naturally, I'm getting ready for bed.'

She had a very valid point, yet it was entirely the wrong thing to have said, because it reminded them both of the bed that was only metres away. His eyes shifted to it, imagining her against the sheets, her hair spread out across the pillows, and his pulse kicked up a notch.

'You should go,' she said barely audibly and, when he looked back at Ms Lawson, she was swallowing so hard her throat was shifting visibly.

'Yes,' he agreed without moving a muscle. It was as though his feet were glued to the ground.

'Mr da Rocha...' She groaned, her nipples so taut

they were pulling at the camisole. His eyes dropped to her breasts and his gut rolled with the sheer force of his desire.

'Salvador!' His name was a plea, a desperate, anguished plea, and that alone finally got through to him. She was begging him to leave and he was standing there, staring at her like an idiot.

'I'm sorry,' he said with sincerity and shock. What the hell had just happened to him? As if finally regaining control of his senses, he forced his feet to move, one after the other, until he was out of her damned suite of rooms and away from the temptation of her beautiful, sensual body.

But it wasn't so easy to put Harper Lawson from his mind. Having ignored his sexual nature for far too long, it had been dragged back to life with an epic bang. A cold shower didn't help, nor did work. When he eventually gave in and went to bed, she filled his head and mind, then his dreams, so he woke harder than granite, so hard it was almost painful to move. And all he wanted to do was reach for her, lift that silk camisole and run his hands over her naked skin, cup her breasts and feel their weight in the palms of his hands. Drag her body against his and kiss her until she was trembling, her pale flesh pink from his stubble, signs of his possession, of his need for her.

He showered again, head pressed against the tiles, eyes closed, trying to focus on work, on anything other than his new assistant, but failing.

So it was with some trepidation that he entered his

office the next morning and only exhaled when he realised she wasn't there yet.

Good.

He moved quickly, shutting the blinds to separate
their workspaces, needing to see more of her like he
needed a hole in the head.

Harper knew he was there, behind the curtains, because he'd had multiple online meetings and his voice
had carried. It was deep, sensual and capable of making her knees tremble even through a wall of glass and
hidden behind a curtain.

Holy heck.

What was happening?

Last night had been surreal and strange and, while
she knew she should be flooded by indignant rage,
she wasn't. He shouldn't have barged in, and he surely
shouldn't have stayed staring at her like he'd never before seen a woman in his life. He'd been completely
transfixed, his expression something she'd never forget.

He'd looked at her as if she was the most desirable
woman on the face of the earth. He'd looked at her as
if he'd wanted to eat her up then and there, and she
couldn't get that out of her mind. She couldn't forget
the way he'd stared, the way his breath had snagged
between his teeth, hissing into the room. She couldn't
forget the way her own body—traitorous, treacherous
body—had responded to him, her breasts tingling, desperate to be touched, moist heat building between her
legs, her heart in overdrive, her mouth not working
properly, her lips full and heavy, aching to be kissed.

It had been a moment of madness for both of them, a strange removal of sense and sanity, the replacement of those things with a primal, physical response that defied logic.

With a pulse that was still none too steady, she flicked up the cuff of her shirt to reveal a tiny tattoo on her inner wrist, a black heart, a reminder to herself that she was her own first love, that she alone was enough. She'd got it after Peter. She still shuddered to think of what a fool she'd been to be taken in by his suave seduction. True, she'd been entirely innocent, with no experience whatsoever in the romance stakes, but she wasn't devoid of all sense, so how come she'd let him make her think she was falling for him? The tattoo was supposed to serve as a reminder that she couldn't trust anyone else with her heart.

Salvador wasn't a contender for that anyway, but it was important to remember her commitment to remaining single. To remember that no man was worth her time—even really, really hot ones.

CHAPTER THREE

'COME WITH ME.'

The words, his voice, pierced her shield of concentration. Harper blinked, disorientated at first, pulling herself, comprehending, out of the documents she'd spent hours reading and back into the office with the beautiful views of the sea. Except there were no views now, because it was night, and she hadn't realised. The office was dark, except for the ultra-bright screen of her computer. It felt like being woken from a long afternoon nap after jet lag, not knowing where she was or when it was.

'Ms Lawson?' His impatience conveyed itself in the tone of his words so she pushed back her chair quickly, moving towards the door, but as she got closer she heard it again—the same hiss of air from between his teeth. And suddenly it all came rushing back to her. The way he'd looked at her. The way his gaze had *felt*. That might seem ridiculous but his gaze had run over her body and had the same effect as if he'd reached out and trailed a finger over her skin.

'I'm here,' she said, voice croaky from misuse.

He flicked on the lights, which should have made

things better but instead made them so much worse, because she realised how close they were standing. She stared up at him and the same sense of disorientation wrapped around her, so it was almost impossible to remember where she was and why she was there. For a moment, the briefest moment, she was just a woman, and he a man, and nothing else had any importance.

His mouth tightened, forming a grim line, but a muscle moved in his jaw. He was feeling what she was, fighting it—this strange, drugging wave of attraction threatening to sweep them both up if they weren't careful.

'You wanted me?' she asked, then cringed inwardly at the unintended *double entendre*.

'I have to talk to you. I also have to eat. Have you eaten?'

Eaten? She frowned. 'Hmm, no.' Not since breakfast, in fact, when she'd grabbed a croissant and coffee and scurried into her office, breathing a huge sigh of relief to have avoided Salvador so successfully.

'Fine. Come with me then.' His eyes pierced hers for a moment longer than was necessary before he turned on his heel and stalked out of her office, into the larger shared space and beyond it to the corridor that led to the rest of the house. She fell into step behind him, glad he didn't wait, glad he didn't look at her, because it gave her some precious, vital moments to pull herself the heck together and remember she was a calm, successful professional in her own right.

The lighting in the house was cosy and ambient, creating a warm, golden glow. He walked down a corridor

Harper hadn't seen before, then onto a terrace set with a table and a single chair, an image that struck Harper right in her centre, filling her with a tangle of emotions.

It just seemed so *lonely*. This man, this house, were so solitary and isolated. Even the house's position, in the middle of a private island surrounded by mountains, rainforest then miles of beaches, made it almost impossible to reach. Everything about his life seemed designed to push people away. Why?

'Ms Lawson will be joining me,' he said, and Harper blinked as the efficient, kind-seeming housekeeper Catarina bustled onto the terrace. She nodded, flicked a small smile in Harper's direction then set to work, placing a second seat at the table and, a moment later, returning with extra cutlery and napkins.

'Dinner won't be long,' Catarina explained to them both, before leaving the terrace.

Harper swallowed. It was ridiculous to feel that the walls were closing in on her when there were no walls out here, yet she felt an oppressive sense of something: emotion; awareness of her own attraction to him; fear of doing something really stupid and showing him how she felt…

It was a balmy, warm night and the air hummed with something like magic. The forest whooshed quietly, the ocean rolled towards them, the moon cut a gleaming path across the dark water, the stars shone and the air was heavy with the fragrance of the island: salt, sand, night-flowering jasmine… It was a wonderful, heady scent, quite unique to this part of the planet, and so, so far removed from the long winter she'd left behind in Chicago.

'Sit down.'

It was impossible to pretend to herself that she didn't find his command even sexier, but Harper couldn't dignify that very primitive response with acknowledgement, and could certainly not leave his tone unchallenged.

'Are you going to order me around all night, sir?' she asked with a saccharine beating of her lashes, moving to the chair and pressing her hand to the back of it.

His eyes flicked to hers, hovering there, momentarily showing surprise, perhaps even uncertainty, before they shuttered any emotion from her view and he was once again impenetrable, impossible to read.

'Please sit down,' he amended with a casual shrug, so she bit back a smile and did as he'd said, pulling the chair back and taking her seat. But the table had been designed for *one*. Adding a second chair was one thing, but it didn't create more leg room beneath it, so the moment he took his seat their ankles and knees brushed. Despite her good intentions, Harper flushed to the roots of her hair, her lips parting as they had last night, heavy with the need to be kissed.

Crap.

Did he feel it too? Or had last night been an aberration, a completely out-of-character moment of distraction that would never be repeated? For Harper, the way he'd looked at her had stirred something deep in her soul, embers of a flame she'd thought extinguished and which, now that it had roared to life, she had no idea how to bank down again.

She crossed one leg over the other, so she took up less physical space, but it was as though his bigger legs, spread wide, exuded a warmth all of their own. So, even though they no longer touched, she felt a static charge brushing her limbs, making it impossible to be aware of anything but him.

'What did you want to talk about?'

'Your work.'

Harper's heart dropped to her toes. 'Is there a problem?'

His frown was reflective. 'Should there be?'

'I— No.' She shook her head and a clump of silky dark hair brushed over one shoulder. She sucked in a deep breath, remembering who she was, what she'd achieved, why she'd sailed to the top of every office she'd ever worked in, and forced a bright smile to her face. Harper had her mother's megawatt-smile lips that were generous and wide, sculpted as if by angels, revealing straight, white teeth. A dimple was gouged in each of her cheeks. It was the kind of smile that invited trust and confidence.

'Go on,' she urged, folding her hands in her lap so she didn't fidget.

'Are you finding everything you need?'

Her brows drew closer together. 'Yes.'

'Because you haven't asked for anything.'

'No.' Her frown deepened. 'Isn't that…wouldn't you prefer that?'

'So long as you are finding what you need, and not fudging your way through things.'

She lifted her eyes heavenwards before she could stop herself, earning a look from him that did funny things to her tummy. His expression darkened, showing disapproval or exasperation—she couldn't tell—but there was something else. Something deep lay within the embers of his irises, something that made her smile drop and her heart go mad.

It was a look that spoke of speculation, of interest. Of the same desire that was thumping through her body, running rampant, begging to be indulged.

She reached for her water glass; it was empty. But a moment later Catarina appeared, brandishing a tray which she perched on the edge of the table so she could remove items, one by one: two wine glasses filled with red liquid, and a platter that overflowed with olives, bread, cheese, oil and some little croquettes.

'That smells delicious,' Harper complimented her honestly. Her stomach gave a rumble of agreement and she laughed awkwardly, pressing a hand to it, so it was the most natural thing in the world for Salvador's eyes to drop lower, skating over the curves he'd stared at the night before, to what he could see of her flat stomach beneath the table.

Harper's mouth went dry, her brain turning to mush. She stared at him helplessly, swimming against the current, trying desperately to hold onto common sense in the face of the most intense physical awareness she'd ever known. With Peter, it had been a slow burn. They'd worked together. He'd been smart and suave, and she'd trusted him. She'd *liked* him. But it had never felt as though every part of her had been struck by lightning. She'd never known anything quite like this before.

'Mr da Rocha,' she murmured, but the words came out breathy, made husky by her desire, so she scrunched up her eyes and tried again. But closing her eyes made her so much more aware of her surroundings: the sound of the forest, the night birds, the rolling, crashing waves, all so elemental and filled with passion; the smell of the tangy night air, the flowers. The island was so wonderfully fragrant and sensual that Harper's skin lifted with goose bumps, the hairs on the back of her neck standing on end.

'Last night,' he said after a beat, and she opened her eyes and stared at him, swallowing past a lump that had formed in her throat, 'Should not have happened.'

He was right, but it still hurt to hear him say that. 'What happened?' she asked unevenly.

His look was disparaging. 'I didn't intend to find you like that.'

Her eyes widened. 'I know.'

'I should have left immediately.'

'It's fine,' she said with a shake of her head. Her body warmed in agreement. She reached for an olive— she was starving—lifting it to her lips and popping it in her mouth. A droplet of oil escaped, so she chased it down her chin with a finger, then stopped when his eyes followed the action with such intensity that she felt he was touching her.

'You live in Chicago.' It was an abrupt change of

conversation and, though it hadn't been a question, she nodded anyway.

'All my life,' she said after a moment, her voice uneven. She reached for the napkin Catarina had brought, wiping her chin, then moved some bread to her plate, breaking it up with her fingers.

'Do you like it?'

'Yes, I suppose so.' She looked around, her lips tugging downwards a little. 'Though it's nothing compared to this.'

He didn't respond.

'This place is…it's so elemental. Here, you could be the last person on earth and there would be more than enough to sustain you.'

He was staring at her as if he could see inside her very soul, but he wasn't replying, so she sighed softly. It was one thing for him to ask questions, but conversation wasn't really possible if he didn't respond to her.

'Do *you* like it?' she asked when he was still just staring at her.

'Like what?'

'Living here.'

His eyes narrowed. 'I haven't thought about it.'

She bit into some bread. 'That's not an answer,' she said after a moment.

'No?'

'No. Even if you haven't thought about it, you could do so now. Think aloud. Ruminate.'

His smile was the last thing she'd expected. In just a flash it was there, like lightning out over the ocean, and then it was gone. But the memory of it danced on her eyelids, and she thought she would say or do almost anything to see that smile again.

'Ruminate?' he repeated, one thick dark brow lifted.

'Sure.'

He looked out to sea, to the streak of milky light cast by the moon. 'I like the privacy.'

She nodded slowly. 'It doesn't get lonely?'

His eyes shifted back to her face, his expression contemplative, so she waited, hands clasped in her lap, breath held, because she really wanted to hear what he had to say. Instead, he reached for his wine and took a sip.

'Mr da Rocha?' she prompted, and his eyes flew back to hers. Some sixth sense told her that he liked her calling him that—liked hearing her use his full name.

'I have staff,' he muttered after a moment. 'I am rarely truly alone.'

And yet, she shivered. There was something in the coldness of his response that made her chest hurt.

'I bet the surfing is amazing.'

'Do you surf?'

She nodded.

'I cannot imagine much opportunity for that in Chicago.'

'No,' she agreed with a smile. 'I take a week off and head to the west coast every summer. I learned as a young girl, and never got over the feeling of being propelled forward by waves. The rush, the power, the connection to the ocean…'

She didn't tell him that it was her father who'd taught her to surf, on the rare weeks he'd remembered he was in fact a father and had flown back into Harper's life. That it was one of the few things he'd given her, that she'd kept as a part of her soul and that, whenever she took a board into the ocean, she felt connected to her dad. A dad who'd deserted her, who didn't deserve a place in her heart, but had burrowed in there nonetheless.

'The waves here are large. I would not recommend you try it.'

'Well, with only a few hours spare in the day, there's not exactly time,' she responded tartly, before remembering she was sitting opposite her boss and that a mite more respect might be called for. She grimaced, lifting her hands. 'I'm sorry.'

She hesitated, then leaned closer so she could study his face better. 'Sir.' His eyes narrowed, his pupils dilated, and she was sure his cheeks had darkened. Her insides stirred and heat built between her legs, so she had to move to uncross then re-cross them. Only his legs were there, beneath the table, and the action brushed them together. The effect was electric. Sparks flew into the air and up into the night sky, like fireworks.

'What for?' His response was gruff, almost a bark.

'Sometimes, I can't help speaking my mind.'

'I don't dislike that quality.'

'Careful,' she said with a half-smile. 'You might not always like what I have to say.'

'Then I'll find a way to punish you,' he drawled, and she startled, because his meaning was impossibly clear, impossibly sensual, and utterly, disastrously desirable.

Her lips parted and his eyes fell to her mouth. This time, she couldn't contain the little moan that escaped, just a whispered sound of attraction. It was all too much.

'I'll be good,' she said quietly, looking down at the table, the dangerous game they were playing tying her stomach into knots.

'Are you good, Ms Lawson?'

She bit down into her lip. 'Oh, yes.'

'Always?'

She didn't tell him about the time she'd been bad. The time she'd screwed up, monumentally, by giving into something not entirely dissimilar to this and going to bed with her boss. Of course, she hadn't known he was married! She'd thought they were falling in love, that the feelings were mutual. But she seriously doubted Peter was capable of love—not for his wife, not for Harper either. She'd learned her lesson. Or had she? Because right now, if Salvador da Rocha snapped his fingers, Harper would go to him in a heartbeat.

What kind of fool did that make her?

'I'm not sure I believe you.'

'Are you calling me a liar, sir?' she asked, and though it wasn't intentional she shifted her legs a little, so now her toe brushed his calf. She had to stop this. It was getting way out of hand.

They had two weeks together, and this was only the second day.

What was going on?

Harper didn't usually do casual flirtation. She didn't do this kind of sexually charged banter. Not anymore.

The relationship with Peter had killed her confidence and destroyed her faith in her own judgement.

His fingers reached for his wine glass, lifting it to his mouth slowly, thoughtfully, then taking a sip. She echoed his movements, tasting her own wine, savouring the flavour while simultaneously recognising she should *not* be adding alcohol into the mix.

'What do you do for fun?' His question was perhaps an attempt to draw the conversation away from the incendiary volley they'd been sharing. Or perhaps he was expecting her to respond with something that would throw fuel on the fire, by responding with an answer that was sensual and provocative.

Harper was drowning. She stared at Salvador, and felt all of her usual reserve and caution drifting away, so she dug her nails into her palm in an attempt to remember who she was and why this was a very, very bad idea.

'I work,' she said, glad that the words emerged reasonably level.

'For fun?'

'Is there something wrong with that? I would have thought it's a hobby we share.'

He frowned, took another sip of wine and Harper exhaled, because things between them were less charged; the provocative verbal game of cat and mouse had moved on. She could relax a little.

Except, with a man like Salvador, she suspected she would be wise never to let her guard down. It wasn't him, but the way she felt about him meant she needed to be permanently cautious.

'I do not consider work fun.'

'Yet you do so much of it?'

He looked beyond her to a point over her shoulder. 'It's habit, I suppose.'

That didn't sound quite right. She was sure there was more to it, but if there was, he clearly wasn't in the mood to expand. She had a little more bread and some more wine, but was relieved when a few minutes later Catarina returned, this time brandishing two plates, each filled with crunchy spiced potatoes, some sautéed greens and what looked to be two excellent pieces of steak.

The smell was immediately mouth-watering and Harper realised she wasn't just hungry, she was famished. She pushed her bread plate to the side to make room, smiling up at Catarina as the woman manoeuvred the plates into position, unaware of the way Salvador's eyes clung to her face, taking in every detail of her smile. Catarina left and Harper's smile dropped, her eyes moving to the meal instead.

'You are a very beautiful young woman.'

She startled, her heart racing. 'Mr da Rocha…'

He held up a hand, but then returned it to the table, reaching for his cutlery.

'You don't…' What could she say? She shook her head, frustrated, hemmed in by her own experiences, her job for this man and a desire that was beating through her like a drum.

'I'm simply observing a fact,' he said, cutting into his steak with apparently no idea how his words had affected her.

'It's not a fact,' she said unevenly. 'When it comes to beauty, there is no such thing.'

'I disagree. Some people, like you, are objectively beautiful.'

It was too much. 'You can't…say that.'

'Did I offend you?'

She shook her head and, for some reason she couldn't fathom, felt the warning sting of tears behind her eyes. She cut her steak quickly, furiously, completely thrown off-balance.

'I was simply observing something about you, in the same way I might say your hair is brown or your nails short.' He lifted his shoulders. 'It was not an invitation to my bed, Ms Lawson. You can relax.'

Relax—after he'd so casually mentioned an invitation to his bed? Did he have any idea how riotous her pulse was? How desperately breathless she felt?

'Stop it,' she said after a moment, shaking her head.

'Stop what?'

'Whatever you're doing. You're…flirting with me, or teasing me, or possibly even toying with me. This working relationship will be much better if you don't do any of those things.'

He leaned back in his chair, studying her, dissecting her, reading her like a book, she feared. 'You don't like to be flirted with?'

'Not by my boss.'

He tilted his head to the side a little, silent for several moments, moments in which she knew he was seeing too much. 'Speaking from experience?'

Damn it! Her harsh intake of breath would undoubtedly give her away. 'I'm not going to answer that.'

'You already did,' he said quietly. 'Not your current boss, I presume?'

The colour drained from her face. 'It's none of your business.'

'So I presume a previous employer. Perhaps the reason you left Stanley Moore Graham after only seven months?'

She let out a shuddering breath. Damn him and his perceptiveness, his quick deductions.

'Your reference from the company was excellent, so it cannot have been a professional problem.'

'I said stop it,' she ground out, her appetite failing her now. She placed her cutlery down neatly and took another sip of wine.

'I'm simply trying to understand you.'

'Why?' she said forcefully, her feelings so wild, she couldn't make sense of any of them. 'Why does any of this matter?'

'I like to know the people who work for me.'

'Now who's lying?' she muttered under her breath.

'Explain.'

Her eyes widened. She hadn't meant him to hear! Cheeks flaming, she glared up at him.

'No.'

He lifted his brows.

'No, *sir*.' She added the title mockingly, but that didn't matter. Even now, when they were sparring, it had the same effect as before, so she knew that it was playing into some kind of fantasy of his, just as it was for Harper. The idea of being made love to by this man, dominated, commanded…

Please, sir…

She closed her eyes on the fantasies that were filling her mind, unwanted, totally unwelcome and definitely unhelpful in the midst of their current conversation.

'Did he break your heart, Ms Lawson?'

She finished her wine in several gulps and replaced the glass a little more heavily than she'd intended.

'That's none of your damned business,' she responded, scraping back her chair. 'Now I see why you always eat alone—you're a terrible dinner companion, Mr da Rocha.' She side-stepped her chair. 'Goodnight.'

CHAPTER FOUR

FOR THE SECOND night in a row, Salvador felt as though a bomb had detonated in the middle of his life. He felt that everything was completely out of control, and he hated that.

But what the hell kind of game had he been playing at? She was right. He'd been flirting with her. Teasing her. Wanting her to flirt back. For no other reason than she did something to him that he liked, something he'd ignored for far too long.

She was stunning, sexy and whip-smart too—he'd checked her work carefully these first two days, not trusting her not to make mistakes. After all, he didn't really know anything about her. But not only had she been faultless, she'd gently corrected other people's errors and she'd reorganised spreadsheets he'd been working from for years, making them easier to read at a glance. She was obviously a phenomenal intellect, a power house, and so far able to keep pace with him without losing her mind.

So why had he teased her?

If he wanted to get laid, he could go to Rio for the

night and find a woman, any woman, to take to bed.
That would be a hell of a lot simpler than this dangerous, complicated flirtation.

Except, Salvador wasn't in the market for a lover.
Losing Anna-Maria and the baby had left Salvador with
a kind of emotional paralysis. He knew he was better
alone.

Whether he desired Harper Lawson or not, giving
into his stupid, masculine impulses would be a short-
cut to disaster.

He couldn't do it.

He needed to be strong for the next twelve nights.
That was all—twelve nights—and then things would be
back to normal. Amanda would be in the office next to
his and Ms Lawson far, far away in Chicago, with her
whip-smart brain and sensual smile charming someone else.

He groaned as the thought of her mouth filled his
mind, as he remembered the way she'd smiled and, even
more dangerously, eaten that olive. The plump flesh had
been pushed between her lips, her eyes closing briefly
as she'd savoured the flavour, and then that glistening
droplet squeezing from the corner of her mouth so that
he'd wanted to lean forward and lick it with his own
tongue, lick her, all over.

Christ.

With the feeling he was fighting a losing battle, he
scraped back his chair and left the table, not returning
to the house, but taking the well-worn path down the
hill towards the beach, in that moment needing to lose
himself in the wildness of the island.

* * *

She'd been hoping the curtains between their offices would be closed again, but no such luck. So, when Harper arrived at her desk carrying a coffee and croissant the following morning, it was to see Salvador already at work, dressed in what she was coming to realise was his uniform: a button-down shirt with the sleeves rolled up, a pair of trousers and socks but no shoes. That small detail did something funny to her heart.

She blinked as he lifted his head, pretending she hadn't seen him, moving to her own desk quickly and flicking the computer to life with fingers that trembled a little. It was impossible not to be aware of him, though, not to feel him as though he were pulsing through the glass. She made a sound of irritation under her breath while waiting for her computer to load, sipping her coffee, then mentally cursing as her eyes strayed to his office of their own volition, definitely without her consent.

This was impossible! How could she treat him normally when she was aware of every little thing he did? She dove into her work, piling through emails first, pulling her hair over one shoulder and toying with it as she read and triaged, responding as needed before moving onto the next.

She was glad to be busy, because eventually the work distracted her, just enough to forget about the man next door—the desire she felt for him, the fact she was so turned on by him, that he'd told her last night she was beautiful, so matter-of-factly, as though he'd simply been remarking on the weather.

But Harper wasn't charmed by that kind of compliment. She'd heard it said to her mother too many times, and always by men who'd broken her heart, so she'd learned from a young age that being admired for looks didn't really equate to much in the end.

She leaned back in her chair and lifted her coffee to sip it, before realising with disappointment that her cup was empty. On autopilot, she stood and moved to the door right as Salvador stepped through, his head bent over a stack of papers he was reading, so she quickly shelved any idea of this meeting being more than a coincidence.

Nonetheless, it brought them both together for the first time since she'd basically stormed out on him last night.

'Mr da Rocha,' she murmured, using her best professional, ice-queen voice, then kept walking towards the coffee machine set up on a bar in the communal area of their office.

'Ms Lawson.' He frowned, looking at her as if from a long way away. Whatever he'd been reading was clearly engrossing.

'I'm just getting a coffee,' she explained unnecessarily, then could have kicked herself for prolonging the encounter. It was as if she couldn't help herself.

'Good idea.' He put the documents down by his side and walked with her to the bar. It was way too small a space for both of them to occupy, given they were sharing it with a cloud of awareness she couldn't shake. Silence fell, an awkward silence, charged and heavy with words unspoken.

'After you.' She gestured to the machine.

'It was your idea,' he said with a lift of his shoulders. 'You go first.'

'No, I—'

'Ms Lawson, we're both too busy to stand here arguing over who gets to use the damned machine first. Make your coffee.'

She flinched, unprepared for the growl in his voice, the tone of his words or the effect they had on her. He was frustrated. Her eyes flew wide as she stared at him, comprehension dawning. It wasn't about the coffee. This was something more—the same drugging need that made it impossible for Harper to sleep or think was overtaking him. Wasn't it? Was it? She could have screamed with annoyance, because she truly didn't know. She suspected so, but everything was so murky. Perhaps it was just her own feelings making it impossible to see his clearly?

She fed a pod into the machine and waited for the liquid to spool out, not daring to look anywhere near his direction. But that didn't matter. She could feel him. She could hear him. Each exhalation wrapped around her, breathed through her, as tantalising and distracting as the rolling waves of the ocean and the salty sea breeze that was gently brushing through the open windows. Birds sang outside, breaking through her fog, or perhaps adding to the magic of what she was feeling.

'All done,' she said, snatching the cup quickly from the machine and turning to leave. Only she turned too fast, without looking properly, and bumped right into Salvador-bloody-da-Rocha's impressive wall of abdominals.

She groaned and pressed a palm to her forehead. *Seriously?*

'I'm so sorry,' she muttered, sounding angry rather than apologetic. After all, he'd been standing too close, he'd been… No. It had been her fault. She'd been so desperate to escape him, before she said or did something really stupid, and instead she'd done this.

She lifted a hand, pressed it to the dark stain spreading across his chest and felt the moment he breathed in, hard and fast, the second her fingers pressed to his shirt. His reaction was unmistakable, the power of that single breath sapping her willpower, her knowledge of what was right and necessary.

'Mr da Rocha,' she pleaded, looking up at him even as he lifted a hand and curved his fingers around her wrist, holding her hand right where it was.

'Yes, Ms Lawson?' he volleyed, his voice steady but slightly off-pitch. She swallowed, her mouth suddenly filled with dust.

'I…' She stalled, unsure what she'd been about to say. 'If you tell me where your room is, I'll go get you a clean shirt. I— That was so clumsy of me.'

'You were running away.'

Her eyes widened at his perceptive, frank assessment.

'Yes.' She couldn't deny it. Her eyes fluttered shut. His grip on her wrist tightened then relaxed, his thumb padding over her sensitive flesh so she was awash with awareness.

'It's smart of you.'

Neither moved. They were so close. If she inched forward just a little, their bodies would be touching. With his eyes still on hers, his hand holding her wrist where it was, he lifted his other to the top button of his shirt and flicked it, effortlessly parting one side of fabric from the other, then the next button and the next, revealing mahogany skin and a sprinkling of dark hair that arrowed towards his trousers.

Oh, good Lord.

Even with one hand holding hers he was able to unbutton the whole shirt and shrug out of one side of it, but as he reached the other he had to let go of her wrist.

It was a turning point. The moment she could have stepped backwards, stung, and quickly left the room. Instead, she stayed where she was, looking up at him, helpless, flooded with desire and desperate to see more of him. She'd dreamed of him for the last two nights, sensual, high-fantasy dreams that had been filled with what she imagined his naked form looked like. But now she had a chance to colour her vision better and she wasn't going to squander it.

Swallowing, she held her ground as he removed the shirt completely and placed it on the counter to his right, where the coffee machine was.

Her eyes followed the action, then returned to his chest, drinking in the sight of him, the beauty of his sculpted chest, his masculine frame and his leanly muscled arms. He smelled woody and spiced, and her stomach churned, the fragrance drawing her in almost as completely as the sight of him.

'You're beautiful,' she said simply, repeating his observation of her from the night before.

His lips quirked into a half-smile then dropped, a look of frustration crossing his face.

'Ms Lawson—'

'I wonder if you shouldn't call me Harper?'

He closed his eyes, as if to push away that very idea.

She swayed forward, unable to stop herself, even when her sensible, rational brain was shouting at her to stop, to remember the awful danger that could come from this. To remember the pain of her past, the embarrassment, the professional limbo she'd found herself in, having had an affair with her married boss.

But this was different. For one thing, Salvador wasn't married. For another, she wasn't so naïve and innocent any more. She'd grown a lot since her affair with Peter. She no longer expected any other person to hold the key to her happiness, and certainly not Salvador. She would be on his island for two weeks. It no longer seemed possible to be here and fight this. So what was the alternative? To quit? To leave him completely in the lurch? Or to stay and accept that something was going to happen, something that was bigger than them, completely out of their control?

'This is not…' he began with a shake of his head, fixing her with a dark stare, a plea in his own eyes. But a plea for what? Did he wish this weren't happening? Or was he asking her to initiate something? Did he feel that, as her boss, he couldn't be the one to act first? Then again, he'd stripped out of his shirt right in front of her.

She licked her lower lip, breath unsteady, eyes finding his.

'Mr da Rocha,' she said, low and huskily. 'I don't know what's happening between us, but it's obvious that neither of us is immune to this…chemistry.' She was pleased to have been able to pluck the perfect word from thin air. After all, what else explained the literal reaction they shared every time they were close to one another?

'And what are you suggesting?'

'That we stop fighting it,' she said quietly, moving closer then, surprising herself with how daring she was being, and how little she cared about going out on a limb like this. She lifted a hand, tentatively touching his chest. There it was—that hiss of breath between his teeth, the sign that he was losing his vice-like grip on any ability to control things.

'That we maybe even give into it.' She blinked up at him, letting her fingers trail his chest now, side to side, swirling circles, feeling his flesh shift beneath her enquiry.

'You work for me,' he pointed out in a voice that was strained by the effort of staying right where he was.

'Yes,' she agreed simply.

'Company policy—'

'Yes. But don't you own the company?'

He frowned. 'That doesn't give me a free hand to disregard Human Resources.'

He was giving her a way out. She should stop this—

surely she wasn't stupid enough to make this mistake again? But it was different. What she'd felt for Peter was nothing compared to the desire ravaging her system whenever Salvador was near.

'I saw the way you looked at me,' she whispered. 'That night and ever since.'

'How do I look at you?' he asked, the plea back in his eyes.

Her lips lifted at one side. 'Like you're wondering if I'm wearing a camisole beneath my blouse. Like you're wondering if I'm wearing a lace thong. Like you want to remove both from my body.'

He tilted his head back, staring at the ceiling. 'You are playing with fire.'

'Aren't we both?'

He dropped his head so that he was facing her once more. 'But you've already been burned.' He lifted a finger, running it over her cheek. She flinched, the words cutting through the desire that had made everything else seem so far away, as if her past was a part of a whole other person's life.

'What?'

He dropped his finger to her chin, then lower to her décolletage, frowning as his finger moved almost against his will to the valley between her breasts and the pearl button there.

'But you're right.'

She swallowed.

'I have been looking at you and thinking, exactly as you said. It is like you read my mind.' Her button came undone easily. She was trembling, completely awash with so many conflicting emotions that the desire he was stirring easily blotted out anything else.

He moved to the next button, and the next, until her shirt parted, as his had earlier. Rather than removing it, he pulled her silk camisole from the waist of her skirt so his hands could touch her bare waist then move higher, his eyes on hers, challenging her, waiting for her to stop him. He moved slowly, so she had ample opportunity to do exactly that, but in truth she wanted him to hurry up, to reach her breasts, to touch them—as she'd been desperate for him to do since the other night when he'd stared at her like a starving man led to a buffet.

She thrust her chest forward and he laughed softly, but it was a laugh devoid of humour, a laugh of surprise, fear and surrender. Then he finally cupped her breasts, feeling their weight in his palms, palms that were rougher than she'd thought they would be—coarse, as if he spent a lot of time outdoors. She didn't care. She liked the contrast of soft and smooth to hard and demanding.

She groaned, tilting back her head, her dark hair forming a curtain down her back, her body quivering at the demanding touch. He felt every inch of her: the underside of her breasts, their curved roundedness and mostly her nipples, which he ran his fingers over at first and then circled, pulled, plucked one by one, then in unison, gently then hard until her knees almost gave way beneath her and the heat between her legs built to an unbearable crescendo. If he was to touch her there, she knew she'd come. Straight away, no further foreplay needed. She was on fire, absolutely exploding with it.

'Mr da Rocha…' She groaned, aware in the tiniest part of her brain that was capable of speech how strange it was to address him so formally even as he gripped her breasts like this. But, hell, there was also something incredibly hot about it. God, how she needed him.

'I want you,' she said boldly. 'I need you.'

She knew he felt the same. He was standing close enough to feel the evidence of that desire pressed hard against her belly. He could take her here and she wouldn't care. Just so long as she got to feel him inside her. It had been too long since she'd been with a man—since Peter, that snake, her only lover—and suddenly she was desperate to erase him from her body, to take that privilege from him of having been the only man she'd made love to.

It was a fever pitch of need that overcame her, so she wasn't aware of the way Salvador had straightened and was staring down at her, as if from a long way away or as if awakening from a dream.

He dropped his hands quickly, as if the flames inside her had leapt through the air and burned him—burned him and pained him.

'You need to leave.' The words were crisp, his voice rumbling as it rolled into the room. Harper stared at him, not understanding. It didn't make sense. Nothing made sense. She was still trembling with desire, playing with one hand behind her back because her mind wouldn't cooperate. She had no idea what he meant.

'You need to leave,' he enunciated more clearly.

Her pulse was jerky for another reason now. Something strange was happening to her, a wave of nausea, anger and self-directed fury. She stared at him, trying to work out what had happened.

'This cannot, will not, happen. Get the hell out of my office now, Harper.' He glared at her with so much anger that she trembled. 'Now.' And then, closing his eyes, he dragged a hand through his hair. 'Please.'

It was the last word that got through to her. Something else was going on, something serious. Something she didn't understand. With legs that were barely strong enough to support her, she turned and ran, not bothering to button up her shirt, simply clutching it together and hoping like hell she didn't run into any household staff on the way.

She didn't—*thank heavens for small mercies*. In the sanctuary of her suite, she slammed the door shut and pressed her back against it while waiting to catch her breath and hoping, desperately, to erase the last stupid minutes from her life.

CHAPTER FIVE

GROWING UP IN the suburbs of Rio de Janeiro had given Salvador a handy vocabulary of curse words and he employed each and every one now as he took the steps to the beach two at a time, running as if a demon were at his back.

He ran to escape—but there was no escape from what had just happened, from what would have happened if he hadn't finally grabbed hold of himself. There was no escaping what he wanted, despite having come to his senses—some of them. But she'd been right there, so tantalisingly close, so perfect, so angelically beautiful and, heaven help him, he'd wanted to reach out and take her then and there against the glass walls of his office.

The image of that dragged a powerful groan from his chest. He ran until he reached the sand, hot and white, shimmering in the mid-afternoon sun. He stopped running, letting the heat flame his feet, the pain a worthy punishment for the dangerous game he'd willingly entered into and very nearly lost control of. *Hell.*

At the water's edge, he stopped just long enough to

remove his trousers so he could stride into the water, the feeling of it a balm against his skin, a necessary dousing of passion. He didn't care about anything then, only this—only a need to come back to himself, to remember his life, his wife, the promise he'd made to himself when she'd died.

He pushed out deep into the ocean, his stride powerful, his legs kicking him away from his home until finally he could no longer stand. He turned onto his back a moment, staring up at the sky, wondering how many times he'd done this while his wife and friend had lain dying, withering into nothingness inside his home. He'd floated in the ocean like this and cursed the heavens, fate, had wished he could save her, begged to switch places with her, offered himself to God, as if it would have made a difference.

Nothing had.

Day by day, she'd grown weaker. He'd watched, held her hand. Had made her empty promises, offering platitudes they both knew to be fake, such as 'You'll be okay…you'll beat this'. Her survival had become his personal quest, the most important thing to him—in those last few months, even more important than the business he'd built almost from scratch. He'd relied on Amanda then, on her professionalism and intellect, her compassion and understanding.

He floated in the water for a long time, staring up at the sky, remembering his wife, the baby they'd lost and the pain of that moment.

Ever since she'd died, he'd been here, single, alone… But not lonely, when Anna-Maria's ghost was everywhere. So too the ghost of his own failure to save them both—his wife and their daughter.

Finally, when he'd ordered his thoughts and remembered his priorities, he swam to shore, his arms just as powerful on the way back, his purpose clear in his mind.

None of this was Harper Lawson's fault and he owed her one hell of an apology.

Harper heard Salvador return but didn't look up. She couldn't. She was still mortified by what had happened, by how brazen she'd been. Only…she hadn't really been, had she? He was the one who'd removed his shirt. But only after *she'd* run her hands all over his chest, practically begging him to take it further.

She closed her eyes on a bitter wave of regret, wondering what the hell had come over her, needing to understand how she'd been so possessed, so utterly mad. They'd both played their part. They'd both wanted… She was sure of it. Yes, she could remember the way he'd been. He'd wanted her too—just not enough.

'Ms Lawson?' His voice had her startling in her seat, the flames she'd thought embarrassment had extinguished kicking into gear.

'Yes?' She didn't look up from her work. He crossed the office, smelling of the ocean. He'd changed—he wore a different shirt with no coffee stain, and a different pair of trousers too. His hair was wet, slicked back from his face. He'd been swimming, she guessed. Yes, there was sand at his temple, a smudge, wiped there without his realisation. Her fingertips ached to reach up and brush it away.

'Can we talk?' He stood beside her, arms crossed, imposing and so handsome.

She lifted her shoulders in a small shrug. 'I suppose we should.'

He reached past her and flicked off her screen, demanding her full attention, so she turned slowly in her chair, lifting her face to his.

'I owe you an explanation.' He said the words with a frown, as though he was surprised to find himself in a position of owing anyone anything.

'Okay.' She bit down on her lip, waiting for him to continue.

'You are a very attractive woman,' he said slowly after a beat, his brows close together. 'And it's obvious that I'm interested in you. What did you call it? Chemistry? Yes, we have chemistry,' he muttered, with something like disgust.

Harper frowned.

'Do you know anything about me, Ms Lawson?'

She pulled a face, considering that. 'I know you own the company,' she responded tartly, earning a look of impatience from Salvador.

'Do you know about my wife?' The words were wrenched from him, but she didn't hear his pain, only his mention of a wife. Suddenly it was history repeating itself, the moment of realisation that she'd been with another woman's husband. She made an awful noise, like an animal in pain, and lifted her hand to her lips, eyes immediately filling with tears.

'I didn't know! Oh, my God, I didn't know. I...
Where is she?'

His lips were pressed together, his skin pale, and
was it any wonder? She'd basically seduced a married
man! Okay, he'd gone along with it, but she'd been so
completely blown away by their shared desire that she
hadn't stopped to think! Beyond the fact he didn't wear
a wedding ring, she'd made no effort to ascertain his
marital status. How could she have been so stupid, so
bloody foolish? But *surely* she would have heard that
Salvador da Rocha was married? Nothing made sense.

'She died.' The words were spoken quietly, and her
heart was racing so fast, so loud in her own ears, that
at first she barely heard what he'd said. But slowly the
penny dropped, the horror of that admission cutting
through to Harper, who lifted her gaze to his face and
saw the anguish there, the pain, and realised it was all
so much worse. 'A little over a year ago,' he continued,
though she hadn't asked. And then, for good measure,
'Cancer.'

'Oh, Salvador,' she mumbled. It was no time for the
formality of his surname. 'I'm so sorry. I had no idea.'

His Adam's apple bobbed as he swallowed, emotions
obviously rolling through him.

'So you can see why I'm not in the mood to get involved with another woman, can't you?'

It was so sad, and such a shock, she found it impossible to know how to respond at first, so she simply nodded slowly while letting his words sink in.

He'd been married.

He'd loved someone enough to marry. And then she'd died.

'I don't— How come I've never heard your wife mentioned.'

His lips were a grim slash in his handsome face, his skin paler than usual. 'Our relationship was not publicised. She preferred it that way.' His eyes assumed a faraway look for a moment, as though he was reliving a long-ago pain. 'Still, it's no huge secret. I presumed gossip might have reached your ears.'

She shook her head sadly. It was all so awful, so tragic. Suddenly, Salvador wasn't just a rude jackass, but a guy who might have been perfectly nice once upon a time, until life came and messed it all up. She stood, because she could no longer sit, and moved close to him because it felt as though that was where she had to be.

'Salvador,' she repeated, though what else could she say? She searched for something, anything, and finally heard herself whisper, 'Thank you for explaining.'

He left her office without another word.

Something about his confession changed everything. Harper had gone from feeling as though she had to fight what was happening between them to understanding why she needed to respect his decision to stay single, while no longer seeing a reason to avoid him.

She was interested in him. Interested in what made him the success he was, in what made him tick.

And it had nothing to do with sex.

Well, that was what Harper told herself as she walked out onto the terrace a little past eight that night to find

Salvador sitting at the table alone, holding a single glass of red wine, no meal there yet.

'Hello.' Her voice was soft, but he turned immediately. Almost as though he'd been waiting for her.

His eyes flicked over her, there was a ghost of a smile and then, 'I eat alone, remember?'

'You live alone,' she corrected quietly, moving to the seat she'd occupied the night before. 'That doesn't mean you have to spend every minute of the day without company, does it?'

His eyes met hers and held, locked in a silent challenge, each waiting for the other to back down, then finally, reluctantly, he gestured to the seat opposite.

'If you wish.'

She did wish. She couldn't say why, but it just *felt* right and, despite everything she'd sworn to herself since things with Peter had ended so disastrously, she followed those instincts now.

Maybe it was the line he'd drawn in the sand, making any relationship off-limits. Maybe that meant she could relax her guard a little because nothing would happen? Despite the tension that still hummed between them, they'd cleared the air, acknowledged what was holding him back—what would continue to hold him back—which meant they could just be together like normal people. Two weeks was a long time to go without any kind of conversation, anyway.

Harper took the seat opposite and barely flinched this time when their legs brushed beneath the table.

'Have you been swimming today?' she asked, because they needed to start a conversation somewhere.

His eyes flickered, then a short nod. 'Yes.'

She looked towards the night-cloaked beaches. 'Which way?'

He hesitated for so long, she thought he simply might be going to ignore the question, but then finally he dipped his head. 'The best beach for swimming is a small cove to the west.' He pointed that way. 'There is a path over there that leads to the stairs.'

'If there's time tomorrow, I might go down. Just to take a look.'

He was silent. Disapproving? After all, this wasn't a holiday, and nothing had changed since that first morning when he'd told her he expected her to be at his beck and call almost all day and night.

'I'll take my laptop, obviously.'

His throat shifted as he swallowed, then Catarina appeared, abruptly ending their conversation.

'Good evening, miss.' Catarina smiled warmly, simply, and Harper felt something like gladness. He didn't quite live alone. True, these people with whom he surrounded himself with were staff, but they were still people. At least there was some interaction.

'Hi, how are you?' Harper returned the smile as the older woman rearranged some things on the table.

'Very well, thank you, miss.' Harper was almost sure she saw the older woman wink as she turned to leave. A few minutes later, she returned with two glasses of wine, as she had the night before, and a platter of the same sort of delicious morsels.

'I'm glad you came out here,' Salvador said after a few moments of silence.

Harper's chest whooshed. 'Oh?'

'I was going to come and find you after dinner, to talk to you. About work,' he added quickly.

Beneath the table, she balled her hands, a nervous reaction. 'If you're worried that what happened between us is going to affect my work, it won't. I promise.'

He studied her face and her heart sank.

'You're not seriously thinking this is going to be a problem?' She had visions of being packed off the island, sent home, no more working for this dynamic self-made billionaire, no incredibly generous bonus, no more once-in-a-lifetime experience on this stunning private island. She had to think fast. 'It meant nothing, Mr da Rocha. It was just a moment, for God's sake.'

His expression was impossible to read and that was the most unnerving thing of all. In their office space earlier, she'd felt more connected to him than she'd known possible. She'd felt as though he could have a thought and she would hear it, but now he was like a stranger, so cold and formal across the table, so careful not to touch her at all.

'I appreciate that,' he agreed with a dip of his head.

'But you're going to fire me anyway?'

He reached for his wine, took a sip, then returned the glass to the table. 'Apart from the fact that would be breaking about a dozen employment laws, I have no reason to fire you, Ms Lawson. I judge people only on relevant metrics and your work is exceptional. That's all that matters to me.'

'Oh.' A warm flood of pleasure ran through her. 'Is it?'

'Looking for compliments?' he asked, his expression lightly mocking, so her stomach rolled.

Before she could demur, he continued regardless. 'You are efficient, intelligent, calm and capable. I can see why Amanda insisted you take over for her.'

Harper's smile glowed with all the warmth of her soul. 'I was so glad she suggested it. I've been in my role for two years and there are times...' She stopped talking, as if belatedly realising she was speaking to the owner of the company.

'Yes?'

It was hard to believe he'd report her for expressing a hint of very normal dissatisfaction, having just praised her so fulsomely. Still, she chose her words with tact and care. 'I know what I'm doing,' she said with a shrug. 'The first three months were thrilling. Learning new things always is. Now, the office runs like clockwork and I could do my work mostly in my sleep. I relished the idea of this challenge.'

'I'm a challenge?' he prompted with a twist of his lips.

'I'm not going to lie to you. Amanda did tell me it would be the hardest two weeks of my life.'

His laugh was soft and short but the sound was like music to Harper's ears. Deep and throaty. She wanted to hear more of it.

'Are you looking for a new job?'

The question surprised her. 'No.'

'Even though you're bored?'

'The money's too good,' she said with a shrug. 'Better than any other executive assistant salaries in Chicago.'

'You'd earn more in New York.'

'Cost of living would go up too, though. Besides, I live in Chicago. I'm not looking to move.'

'It's not a huge move. Or there's the west coast,' he pointed out. 'Get a job in a tech giant?'

'Are you trying to get me to quit?' she asked, only half-joking.

His frown was reflective. 'No. I was...' Catarina appeared again then, bustling to clear their bread plates and make space for the impending main course. 'I was offering suggestions based on what I thought might suit you better.'

'Thank you,' she said, recognising a fellow problem-solver. But he didn't have all the information: her problems weren't so easy to solve. 'But I have a life in Chicago. Family.' She didn't want to go into specifics; she never did. 'I can't leave.'

He studied her for so long, she felt the familiar ratcheting up of tension, the desire they'd been fighting swarming her anew so her throat was dry and she could hardly swallow.

'Perhaps another job in the company?'

'I have one of the most senior executive assistant roles.' She shrugged. 'But thanks. I'll keep my eyes open.'

'Did you ever consider another career?'

She almost flinched. The question was far too close to home. For a flash of time, she imagined how her life might have turned out if her mum hadn't got sick. She saw college life, the degree she'd been accepted to do, the career she might have had, sitting on the other side of the desk, making the decisions rather than just greasing the wheels to allow those decisions to work. But it wasn't possible.

'No.' A flat denial was easier than explaining the truth. She looked away out to the ocean, straining to hear the waves. 'What was it you wanted to talk to me about?'

'I have to go on a trip, leaving the day after tomorrow. I'll send you an email with the details. Amanda usually coordinates with my flight crew to manage the jet. Did she leave you notes about travel?'

She had left notes, copious notes, but had assured Harper they weren't likely to be needed. She'd said Salvador only had one trip on the horizon and that was over a month away.

'I have the notes,' was all Harper said. 'Where will you be travelling to?'

'We,' he corrected with a frown, as though that was the last thing he wanted. Her gut twisted at the idea of more travel and, yes, there was a small part of her that was excited about the thought of travelling *with* Salvador. Cursing her juvenile reaction, she focussed on the business side only.

'To Zakynthos, Venice then Prague.'

She blinked. 'Is that all?'

'It will be a quick trip. Two, three days at the most.'

'Three cities in two days?' She tried not to acknowledge her disappointment. This wouldn't be a holiday.

He nodded. 'I need to view some properties.'

That sparked her interest. 'You can't just tour virtually?'

'I've done that.' He nodded. 'But I believe in the importance of feel. Going somewhere, seeing it in person, smelling the air, hearing the noises, watching locals—these things help me decide if something is a good investment.'

'What kind of properties?'

Catarina returned with dinner—rice, chicken and vegetables. It smelled delicious.

He regarded her a moment. 'It's a chain of hotels.'

'Oh, nothing major, then,' she responded with a hint of a smile.

An answering smile twisted her tummy into knots.

'You can make the arrangements?'

'Of course.' This was probably the task most like any she'd done in her other roles. 'Email me any specifics and I'll handle it.'

Harper Lawson was someone who kept her cards close to her chest by force of habit, he suspected. Whenever she began to speak freely, she stopped herself, changed subject and spoke a little more slowly, as if hearing what she was about to say before she said it.

She was careful with what she said, but her face was so expressive, her eyes so telling, that he understood far more than she probably would have wanted.

He'd seen sadness, for instance, when she'd spoken of her family. And desperation, when she'd briefly mentioned her salary, her need for a high-paying job. There was also her pragmatic assessment of the prospects of New York—it had all been an equation of income and outgoings, no thought of the beauty and pace of that city, of how she might enjoy living somewhere new. It had been the same with the west coast. Despite the fact a move there would take her to the beaches she obviously loved so much, she hadn't shown even a flicker of remorse about it not being right—because of her family in Chicago, which caused her sadness.

There was also the way she'd shut him down when he'd asked about alternative careers. *No.* Then a swift change of subject, refocusing on the business at hand. Which made him believe that in fact there had been something else she'd wanted to do at some point, and yet she hadn't pursued it.

He had gleaned all this from a few minutes' conversation and, though it was none of his business, he found himself wondering about her later that night as he worked propped up in bed, coffee on the bedside table, laptop on his thighs.

It had been the kind of day he'd rather forget.

But it had also been a day filled with memories that he kept looking at, indulging in, even when he should know better. The way she'd felt, pressed up against him. The feel of her breath against his cheek, her parted lips, her breasts… God, her breasts. The way her nipples had hardened beneath his touch, her head thrown back, her silky hair smelling like citrus blossoms, making him ache for her on every level.

It had been way too long, that was all. He'd been celibate for almost two years. Since that one night with Anna-Maria, when they'd conceived Sofia.

Their teeny, tiny little daughter.

His gut tightened when he remembered that little

face, those shallow breaths, the downy skin and fluffy hair, black like his.

His heart squeezed so hard and tight, the pain so intense he almost felt as though he might die from it. But he wouldn't. He knew that from experience. It was not a new pain, but rather a part of him, stitched into his being every day, with every breath, every memory of that baby, his wife, the lives he'd failed to save.

He'd known pain before. Had known his father's rejection, his mother's sudden death. But nothing had prepared him for the ache that had spread through him when he'd held his baby, his fragile, weak baby, and had been forced to accept that there was nothing he could do.

How did one survive such grief?

He was surviving, but he was changed for ever, unable to live as he had before, with a future he considered his own. He was simply going through the motions of life now—he had no right to expect pleasure, to seek joy of his own. He didn't want that. Numbness was the closest thing to salvation he experienced and he refused to let it go.

CHAPTER SIX

SINCE ARRIVING ON Ilha do Sonhos, Harper had come to appreciate that there was something quite unique about the place. Looking east from Salvador's kitchen was the most exquisite sunrise she'd ever seen, filled with pink and purple that turned to orange as it lightened. In the evenings, from the western courtyard where they'd shared dinner twice now, the sunsets were beyond compare. It was the first time she'd been somewhere that showcased such stunning bookends to the day, the natural phenomena a show she couldn't bear to miss. And it had only been a few days!

There was something about marking the beginning and end of the day in a form of ritualistic light-worship that seemed important to Harper and which was grounding and breath-taking. As her fourth day drew to a close, she studied the pile of work on her desk, knowing she'd need to return to it later that night, but that a short break wouldn't make a huge difference. Stretching her arms over her head, she stood, leaving her office and hovering in the shared space a moment before moving to Salvador's door and knocking once.

He lifted his head, eyes piercing hers, so her heart skipped a beat and the smile she forced felt unnatural.

'I'm going to take a break. Do you need anything?'

His eyes lingered for a moment too long on her face before dropping to her lips then looking away. There was consternation on his features, his lips compressed so her heart kicked up a gear, because she understood.

Whatever he'd said, no matter what they'd agreed, he still wanted her.

The air between them sparked a little. 'No.' A gruff response. 'Thank you.'

It was an attempt to soften his initial answer but it didn't really work. She turned and left quickly before she could do something she'd regret.

She knew the beaches around the island had big waves, because Salvador had told her so, and because she heard them day and night, the pounding of water to coastline reassuring and rhythmic. But the path she followed from the house brought her to a cove that was rounded in shape and perfectly still. A natural wave break had been formed by the shape of the land here, so it was the perfect spot to swim calmly and enjoy the serene ocean.

Harper didn't have time to swim and it was enough to dip her toes in the water and feel the cool balm. She walked to the edge, sighing as she felt the ocean, and closed her eyes. She remembered being a little girl at the beach with her dad, a couple of years after her parents had divorced, her dad so strong and big, his laugh the nicest thing she'd ever heard as he'd hoisted a little Harper onto his shoulders and carried her into the ocean. Her toes had dangled into the sea, pleasantly cool like this, and she'd giggled because it had tickled a little. The deeper her father had gone, the more she'd laughed, until the water was at his shoulder height. She'd been so happy to see him, to have the full force of his attention for a change.

'Ready?' he'd called up to her as a wave came close to his face so he had to turn away.

'I don't know, Daddy.'

'You can do it, Harp Seal.'

She'd loved that nickname, though she hadn't heard it for a long time. Not since he'd left.

'I don't know.'

But she'd wanted to impress her dad, maybe even win him back. So she'd ignored her fear and ground her teeth.

'Okay, I'm ready!'

He'd placed his palms beneath her feet, forming a platform, and then ducked his head forward so she was diving into the water—deep, cold, salty heaven. She'd faced her fears in the hope of showing her dad how brave she could be, but he'd left again anyway, disappearing from her life and leaving only disjointed, unsatisfying memories.

Twenty years later, on a different beach, Harper turned her back on the ocean, sighed softly and made her way back to the house.

He checked the itinerary as a matter of course, but it was perfect. She'd booked a room for each of them in the hotels he'd specified, and had managed to schedule his existing commitments into the new time zones, ensuring his normal work schedule wouldn't be affected by the travel. He noted she'd blocked out half-hour times for herself as well, per their agreement, and not for the first time he wondered about that.

Why half an hour? What did she do with that time? She'd been so adamant about it. It wasn't for food—she ate at her desk. Did she nap in the middle of the day? Possible, but unlikely. She didn't seem like someone who'd nap. Then again, a restorative sleep had been proven beneficial for concentration, and she was certainly incredibly focussed. Or did she disappear to read a book?

He didn't know, but he wanted to, almost as much as he wanted to see her naked, to touch her, to feel her... He dropped his head to his hands on a laugh that was totally devoid of humour.

He'd found himself in some kind of hell and there was nothing he could do about it.

Harper had been brought to the island by helicopter, and they left the same way, but this was an entirely different experience because Salvador took the controls. Harper sat in the back, rather than in the empty seat beside him—he didn't offer that seat to her and she was glad. Even the view she had from there was pantie-melting hot.

He was so in control of such a complex instrument panel. So had the pilot on the way over been, and it hadn't affected Harper like this, but now was different. This was Salvador, the man who ran a multi-bil-

lion-dollar empire, who seemed able to turn his hand
to anything. She sat back in the seat, trying to look out
of the window rather than staring at him, at the tanned
forearms that were exposed by his shirt as he moved
levers and held the flight controls. It was just so incredibly, intoxicatingly masculine...

He landed the helicopter at a private airstrip on the
outskirts of Rio de Janeiro—Christ the Redeemer had
guided the way—and his private jet sat waiting on the
tarmac.

'Are you going to fly this too?' she couldn't help asking as a swarm of staff approached the helicopter, removing luggage, checking controls, greeting Salvador.

Harper had arranged all this, per Amanda's check-
list, but she still hadn't quite known what to expect. The
reality was actually quite unnerving.

'No. On the plane, I work,' he said, the words holding a warning, as though she'd come along just to try
to distract him.

Fine by me, she thought waspishly, falling into step
beside him. But as they approached the steps at the
bottom of the plane he paused to allow her to precede
him, his hand reaching out and touching her lightly
in the small of her back to urge her forward. It was a
nothing gesture, only it didn't *feel* like nothing. Sparks
flew from her back all through her body and ignited the
blood in her veins as though it were lava. She couldn't
help her sharp intake of breath, nor the way her eyes
skidded to his. He kept his gaze resolutely averted, so
she saw only his profile, but his jaw was clenched—she
knew he felt it too.

Whatever feelings inside Salvador had unknowingly given her were usurped by a sense of awe. She'd naturally expected to be impressed by a private jet and yet she hadn't thought it would be quite as opulent as this—from the grey leather seats, each wide enough to outdo a first-class seat in a commercial jet, to the arrangement of them. It was like a trendy bar rather than a plane, the seats facing one another, low coffee tables between them. There was a partition behind this seating area and Harper moved past it, too curious to be polite and wait to be shown.

The next room was a boardroom with a large table and a big screen on the wall at one end. It would easily accommodate up to twenty people. The sense of awe grew as she moved further down the plane, and then something else overtook it completely.

Bedrooms—two of them—each with a huge double bed and *en suite* bathroom.

Her pulse was thready and she spun guiltily, but Salvador was right there. He must have been following her and she hadn't realised. Now they bumped into one another and his hands came out and caught her arms, his expression exasperated and impatient, even when he held on far longer than was necessary to steady her.

She looked up into his face and everything evaporated—common sense, thought, his confession about his late wife, the certainty that they couldn't, shouldn't act on whatever feelings they had. There was only desire now.

But for Salvador this was clearly not the case. He dropped his hands quickly and stepped backwards, irritation in the depths of his eyes. 'The flight is about fourteen hours. You should choose a room.' He gestured towards both of them. 'I'll work from the front of the plane for now.'

'Which room is yours?'

'Generally I use this one.' He nodded to the left.

'Then I'll take the other,' she said. It was right across the aisle from his. *Oh, great.* That wouldn't be a problem *at all*, she thought sarcastically.

'Fine. The staff will bring your luggage through and take your order. If you need anything, let them know.'

'Is that code for "don't bother me"?' she asked before she could consider the wisdom of being quite so pushy.

He smothered a sigh. 'No, Harper. It's not.' She felt like a silly school girl. Biting into her lower lip, she refused to drop her gaze, though, nor to show him how chastened he'd made her feel. 'Have a nice flight.'

The expectation being that he didn't want to see her for the duration, she thought with a little internal harrumph. No shared dinners on board—well, fine. She had stacks of work to catch up on, and her usual video call to her mother as well.

She hadn't been planning to reply but there wasn't the chance anyway. Salvador turned and left before she could open her mouth to say, 'Thank you very much.'

Just knowing she was on board was his undoing. This was getting out of hand. Salvador da Rocha was famed for his control, his willpower, his ruthless determination, but in the last few days he'd come face to face with a slip of a woman who seemed to have the power to undo all of that—just by bloody existing within his airspace!

He shouldn't have brought her, he realised halfway into the flight. She could have run things from the ground on the island, and he could have got some damned respite from her. Maybe he should send her home immediately.

And pigs might fly, he thought with a grimace.

For, as desperately inconvenient as he found the distraction of Harper Lawson's presence, he suspected her absence would be even more of a concentration-killer. He stretched the fingers of his right hand wide, remembering the sparks he'd felt when he'd done something as innocuous as touch her back to board the flight. Even that simple contact had made him feel alive with the power of a thousand watts.

This wasn't going away. He couldn't ignore her: he couldn't ignore the way she made him feel.

But it wasn't really Harper, he consoled himself quickly. It was the fact she was there: a beautiful, intelligent, interesting woman right beneath his nose who'd declared them to have chemistry; who'd made it obvious she was attracted to him; who'd fall into his bed if he allowed it… God. The willpower required to make that not happen!

But what if it did?

What if he gave into this?

A year after burying his wife, one of his oldest friends—what kind of sick son of a bitch did that make him? Only, their marriage hadn't been quite normal. They hadn't married for love, but rather because Anna-

Maria had fallen pregnant. Salvador had been determined not to be like his deadbeat father, refusing to acknowledge his own child, choosing instead to pay off the mother, to silence her. He would never have done that. He'd wanted to be a family, the kind of family he'd never known.

It hadn't been a normal marriage for Salvador but his guilt at not being able to love Anna-Maria in the way she'd deserved as a wife—even as she'd lain dying— was a constant source of pain to him. To move on, and with someone so very fit, healthy and *alive,* would feel like a betrayal of the worst possible kind.

He groaned, pressing his head back against the seat of the plane, scrunching up his eyes and doing his very best not to think of Harper, even as memories and fantasies weaved through his mind like ribbons in a stream.

After the heat of Brazil, Zakynthos was surprisingly cool. Harper had only been away from Chicago for a few days but her body had grown accustomed to the balmy, tropical temperatures. She liked it, she realised. Liked the way the warmth soaked into her skin, her heart, the sea breeze making her feel alive and elemental.

But Zakynthos was stunning, and not just because she was seeing it through the lens of a billionaire's lifestyle. Though that didn't hurt, she thought wryly as she stepped into the back of a large black Range Rover with darkly tinted windows. There was a driver and, though Salvador offered Harper the front seat, she demurred, preferring to sit on her own in the back than feel obliged to make small talk with the driver. Besides, she was staff, and it felt somehow more appropriate. So Salvador took the front seat, his arm resting casually along the side of the door, his fingers drumming a slow, rhythmic beat on the luxury interior. She studied him in the side mirror, which gave her a perfect view of his face, but every now and again his gaze would flick to the mirror, their eyes would meet and it was as though she was being electric-shocked.

Yet she didn't look away.

She couldn't. Not wouldn't—couldn't. It felt physically impossible, despite the stunning scenery of the island that she was aware of in her peripheral vision. Primarily, there was only Salvador and her. Not even the driver entered her thoughts.

After a fifteen-minute drive, the car pulled up onto a sweeping driveway of white gravel, with elegant palms forming lines on either side. At the front of the white-walled hotel, a bougainvillea grew opportunistically, its bright, papery, purple flowers scrambling over every available surface, offering a stark, beautiful contrast to the crisp colour of the walls and the sparkling turquoise ocean beyond.

Everything about the hotel screamed understated luxury, from the grand entrance to the staff waiting by the door dressed in black suits with gold cuffs. They greeted Salvador as though he were royalty, and Harper hovered a little behind, turning to look at the view and inhale, searching for salt and tropical sweetness in the air. While this was beautiful, it was nothing to Ilha do Sonhos, she realised with a thud in the middle of her chest. She'd found heaven on earth, and now even some-where like this couldn't really compete.

'Ms Lawson?'

Salvador's voice made her spine tingle. She turned to him slowly as a gentle breeze caught at her hair so she had to lift a hand to it, to pull it back over one shoulder. He watched her, frowning, then gestured towards the door, impatient, short and something else. Resigned? Her heart quickened and she took a step towards him with the strangest feeling that she was moving head-long into a fate beyond her control.

CHAPTER SEVEN

IT WAS CLEAR that Salvador had no intention of enjoying a single thing about being in Greece. They toured the hotel—he wore a suit, and avoided doing anything so frivolous as even touching the water of the pool. It was a stunning facility. The rooms were clearly luxurious and decadent while still retaining a local character—wide doors, carved windows open to the water and brightly coloured interiors, such as the bed in Harper's room that was a cheery turquoise and the chair by the window which was a glossy yellow.

The floors were tiled, big, terracotta squares that were cool beneath the feet. Rugs had been added for comfort in some areas. It was sublime. Harper's room had the most amazing view, but she knew from having arranged Salvador's accommodation that his suite included a small infinity pool. She could only imagine what the outlook would be from there in the evening. How would the sunsets here compare to those of the Ilha do Sonhos?

Her lips pulled to the side and she realised, with heat

rising in her cheeks, that Salvador was looking at her, waiting for her to respond.

Furious with herself for having missed something, she forced her concentration back to the tour. 'I'm sorry. What was that?'

'Is something the matter, Ms Lawson?' he asked, curtly, so her embarrassment grew, particularly as they weren't alone—the manager of the hotel was standing nearby, pretending not to hear the interchange.

'No,' she whispered back with a hint of anger. 'I'm fine.'

'Then perhaps you wouldn't mind paying attention? I didn't bring you along to stare off into space.'

She could have slapped him. Anger sizzled in her veins, all the stronger because of her general sense of frustration and thwarted need.

'Yes, sir,' she replied through gritted teeth, pleased when the volley hit its mark. His own cheekbones slashed with a hint of colour, his chest moving as he sucked in a breath then turned away from her.

'Go on,' he commanded the manager, who was running through the latest occupancy figures. Harper made a show of removing her phone, loading up a document and taking notes for the rest of the tour—particularly useful as it gave her an excuse to avoid Salvador's eyes. But, as they returned to the foyer of the hotel, the manager—whose name Harper had uncharacteristically missed—turned to them both, his gaze lingering a little longer on Harper's flushed face.

'The bar is an excellent place to cool down,' he said,

with a smile that lasted a second too long, his body a little close to Harper's.

'We have work to do,' came Salvador's clipped reply.

Such was Harper's simmering rage, and now resentment at being spoken for, that she pushed an over-sweet smile onto her face and waved it in Salvador's general direction. 'But afterwards a drink would be lovely. What do you recommend?'

'The hotel has a speciality cocktail; you cannot leave Zakynthos without trying it.'

'Well, that sounds like important research,' she cooed, pleased to feel the glowering presence of Salvador at her side.

'But, as this is not a vacation, this is not the time.'

'Later.' Harper increased the wattage on her smile. This time, when Salvador put his hand in the small of her back, it wasn't as light or gentle as earlier, but the effect was the same, or perhaps stronger. Sparks, flames, fire, fury sizzled inside her body, turning her into a fantastic mess of lava and lust.

He guided her towards the bank of lifts. 'I can walk,' she muttered. He didn't remove his hand and she was glad. The feeling of his fingers splayed wide and possessively was so much more than a simple direction. This was something more—something primal and virile, something that showed his emotion.

The lift doors opened and she stepped in, pulling away from his hand and pressing her back, tingling and warm, against the lift wall. Because if he touched her for a second longer she knew she'd ignite.

'What the hell is going on with you?' she snapped. 'You were so rude to that guy.'

'Because I wasn't batting my eyelids and begging him to buy me a drink?' Salvador responded, staring at her across the expanse of the lift.

'I was just being nice because you'd been such a jerk!'

'A jerk!' he repeated, nostrils flaring. 'I was business-like and professional. There is nothing wrong with that.'

Harper rolled her eyes. 'And how about the way you spoke to me?' she demanded. 'I have done everything you've asked of me, worked day and night non-stop since I came into your life—'

'I told you, that's the job!' he responded with a raised voice.

'Yes, yes, you told me,' she said, mortified to feel the warning sting of tears in the back of her eyes. She refused to give into them and bit into her lower lip until the sensation passed. 'But I have done it, without complaint, and the first moment my attention wandered for even a moment you acted as if I've made some fatal error. You deliberately embarrassed me in front of him!'

Salvador stared at her, darkly complex emotions chasing themselves across his face. Harper made a noise of frustration and then relief when the doors opened to her floor and she could step out.

But Salvador was right behind her, his stride long. 'You're not on this floor,' she reminded him through gritted teeth.

'We're not done!'

'Oh, yes, we are. I have nothing else to say to you right now.'

'Your mind did wander,' he said, not heeding her warning. 'You were distracted.'

'And you were rude about it,' she replied, not looking at him.

'What should I have done?'

'There are a million ways you could have brought me back into the conversation without making it seem as though I'm some incompetent—'

'That wasn't my intention.'

'Wasn't it?' she shouted, then squeezed her eyes shut as emotions rolled through her again. 'You've been acting like I've done something wrong, like you're angry with me. And maybe you are, but if you're angry it's because of what happened between us. And that's not my fault.'

He was close now, so close. She swiped her key card over the door but it didn't work. Her fingers were shaking. She tried again and the light flashed red. Harper cursed silently.

'Allow me.' His voice was gruff, hoarse, those same dark emotions she'd seen on his face evident in his tone now.

'I can do it,' she snapped, pulling her hand away from his.

'Damn it, Harper, for crying out loud, this isn't a big deal.'

'It is to me.'

'You're overreacting.'

She whirled around to face him but, just as on the

plane, he was right behind her and this time there was a door at her back, so she was all but trapped between Salvador's rock-hard chest and the door's firmness at her spine.

'Don't tell me I'm overreacting,' she said unevenly. 'You made me feel… You treated me…' She glared up at him but, close like this, it was almost impossible to hold onto her anger. She needed it, like a shield to keep her safe. 'You're a jerk,' she repeated.

'Yes.' His eyes narrowed, his pupils huge in his golden eyes. She swallowed, staring up at him, unable to look away, barely able to breathe. 'I know.'

'So how about you try not to be?'

'And then what happens?' he asked darkly, leaning closer. 'What if I tell you I think you're the smartest person I've ever known?' She gasped. 'What if I tell you I'm blown away by your attention to detail, your planning, your reporting?'

Her heart thumped hard into her rib cage, his praise like warm treacle on her flesh. Of their own volition, her hands lifted to his shirt, pressing to the starched fabric there, the fabric that had seemed so incongruous by the pool, when they'd been surrounded by happy holiday makers, but which now felt like the best thing ever.

'Are you?'

'Yes.' The word was a whip in the air between them. 'I think my admiration is very obvious.'

She snorted. 'Yes, of course, how silly of me not to realise when all you do is berate—'

He pressed a finger to her lips. 'Once. And it won't

happen again.' Their eyes met and something passed between them. 'I'm sorry. I was…'

'Frustrated,' she mumbled against his finger, eyes blinking up at his. When he didn't remove his finger, she pursed her lips, kissing it, and when he still didn't pull away opened her mouth to take the tip between her lips just a little way. Nerves were flooding her, because it was so out of character to act like this, and at the same time it felt so *right* and *normal*, as though she had no choice but to act on the feelings that were pulling her towards him.

Salvador groaned, dropping his head forward.

'Yes,' he said unevenly after a moment. It took her a second to realise he was agreeing that he had indeed been frustrated.

He pulled his finger out of her mouth, but not far. He let it rest on her shoulder and slowly, as if a magnetic force were drawing Salvador down and he was desperately fighting it, his head dropped lower and lower, hers tilting upwards until their lips met. It was like a thousand lightning bolts had speared the earth around them.

Harper felt it all through her body, in the air, in the way Salvador shuddered, the kiss shifting tectonic plates and everything in between.

His mouth was firm and insistent, just as she would have expected, his trademark confidence meaning he kissed arrogantly, demandingly, and it was incredible. She surrendered to the kiss, her lips parting beneath his, her hands bunching in his shirt, the power of that connection burning her to the tips of her toes. His tongue flicked hers hungrily and she kissed him back, tangling their tongues, her hands moving from his shirt to the back of his neck, fingers curling in the hair at his nape, her breasts crushed to his chest where her hands had been, her thighs pressed to his.

His body pushed forward so the door was hard at her back, and she was aware of every inch of his muscular frame. The hardness of his groin made her breathless with need, stars of desire filling her eyes, every bit as bright as the night sky on Ilha do Sonhos.

She kissed his name into his mouth, delighting in the way it tasted, in the feel of his hands on her body as he kissed her senseless and breathless.

And then he stopped, pulling away from her, his eyes glittering when they met hers, his expression hard, shocked and possibly even afraid.

He swore under his breath, staring at her, breath uneven, and she stared back, the world tilting off its axis and everything moving beyond her control.

'Do you see why I cannot say nice things to you, Harper?' he demanded, his hands impersonal now as he straightened her clothes, tucking her shirt back into her skirt.

Hurt, she pushed his hands away, face pale. 'I can do it.'

Taking his lead from her, he took a step backwards, hands on hips. 'Nothing good can come from this. I wish you wouldn't—'

'Don't blame me, don't you dare,' she said. 'None of this is my fault.'

'Isn't it?' he responded, and she had no idea what that meant.

'What did I do wrong, then?' she demanded angrily.

'You came into my life.'

'Gee, thanks.' She blinked down the hallway, her face pale. 'Do you really feel that way? Do you want me to leave? Because I will. I'll go back to Chicago if you'd prefer.'

'What I would prefer is never to have met you.'

She frowned, wondering at the soreness in her chest, the ache that was spreading through her whole body.

'Forget what I said earlier,' she muttered, spinning away from him and trying her key card once more. She could have cried tears of relief when it worked and the door sprang open. 'You're not a jerk. You're an A-grade asshole and I can't wait to see the back of you.'

She'd never been more satisfied to slam a door in her life.

He'd overreacted.

Royally.

She was right—he'd acted like an asshole.

But if he hadn't stopped what had been happening between them, he would have stripped her naked and taken her right there in the corridor of the hotel. He wracked his brain, staring out at the stunning view from his hotel room, trying to remember what life had been like before Anna-Maria. He'd had lovers—lots of lovers—but had he ever felt an almost demonic need to possess a woman? Had he ever been driven so wild?

His features were grim, his body tense.

If he had, he'd forgotten over time, because the way he'd responded to Harper in the corridor outside her

room had felt like a first to Salvador. And a last. It had
to be the last. He couldn't keep succumbing to temptation just because she was there, just because he wanted
her with the might of a thousand gods.

Every incendiary touch just reminded him of how
he'd failed Anna-Maria. Failed to respond to her, to
want her beyond that first night. Even to love her as
she'd deserved to be loved—not as an old friend, but as
a lover and wife. And, the worst failure of all, he hadn't
been able to save her or their daughter.

With a groan, he dove into the water of his pool,
holding his breath under water, willing himself to push
Harper from his mind just as easily as he cut through
the pool and emerged on the other side. Would that it
could be so easy.

Venice was not much better. Another stunning hotel,
this one on the Grand Canal and with no pretensions to
'rustic charm'. It was the very last word in glamorous
luxury, from the enormous marble keystone tiles to the
golden chandeliers and curving timber staircase that sat
grandly in the entrance foyer. At this hotel, their rooms
were side by side—which would have made it harder to
ignore him except for the fact they'd barely spoken two
words since that kiss in Zakynthos. They'd exchanged
emails as necessary, and Harper had tagged along to his
meetings, nodding her agreement when he'd asked her
to do various tasks, but that had been the extent of it.
The flight had been conducted in silence—Harper had
gone to her bedroom to work, stony as she'd passed him.

At least, she'd looked stony, but her insides had been

quivering and melting, the memories of their kiss driving her almost crazy. Even sleep offered no respite: he was there, his hands on her body, his lips on hers, the kiss so perfect, so hot and demanding, so satisfying. She'd known how perfect it would be for him to come into her room…but she couldn't think like that.

This was a disaster. Harper had become so caught up in how she wanted him that she had forgotten how committed she was to avoiding entanglements. There was nothing simple and uncomplicated about Salvador. He was an emotional wreck, someone she needed to avoid like the plague.

They'd arrived in Venice mid-morning and toured the hotel first, then headed into a meeting with one of the representatives from the consortium selling the chain of hotels. Harper's head was swimming after those three hours—the figures discussed, the terms agreed to; it was all so much, such big business. She hadn't really appreciated how much of this Salvador conducted personally, but of course it was his company, and he was known for taking a hand in all his dealings.

The flame of curiosity burned a little brighter in her chest, because her desire to learn about him hadn't abated, but she wouldn't give him the satisfaction of asking questions.

When the meeting was over and she was walking alone through the hallway, her heels making a reassuring clackety-clack sound on the floor, he caught up with her.

'Ms Lawson.' The way he said her name was a command to stop walking, but she didn't. 'Harper.' The second was said more sharply but she gasped, because the only other time he'd used her first name had been with his mouth pressed to hers. She spun to face him, eyes flashing anger.

'What?'

'What?' he repeated, brows raised.

'I'm sorry,' she said with sarcasm. 'What would you like, sir?'

A muscle jerked in his jaw. 'Have dinner with me.'

'But you eat alone,' she reminded him tartly.

He crossed his arms over his chest. 'Have dinner with me tonight.'

In Venice, of all places. 'Is this work? Are you ordering me to?'

'Ordering you?' he repeated incredulously. 'No, I'm not ordering you to. I'm…asking.'

She was dumbfounded. How dared he? He was blowing hot and cold with her, her not knowing what he wanted from one day to the next, and she wasn't going to be jerked around by him any more.

'Oh, good,' she murmured. 'Then my answer is no. Thank you,' she added for good measure, flashing a false smile before turning and stalking away. There was no door to slam this time but she still felt damned satisfied by her hasty retreat.

He watched her walk away with a strange feeling in the pit of his gut and an anger that was completely self-directed. Why the hell had he done that? After having drawn a line between them in Greece, why invite her for dinner? Because he was a fool and needed to learn his lessons many time over? He made a disgruntled sound of impatience, aware that his body was poised to follow Harper even when he knew it was the last thing he should do. He hated the silence that existed between them, that was why. He hated being near her and not talking. Not hearing *her* talk. But silence was still better than the alternative, so why not let sleeping dogs lie?

It was as though a fever overtook him every time they were together, and he hated it.

What he needed was to make it through this trip without making another Harper Lawson related mistake, and get back to the relative safety of Ilha do Sonhos.

He was still staring at Harper, without realising it, as she approached the lifts. Perhaps he was willing her to look back at him because, as the doors opened, she angled her head, their eyes met and Salvador had the strangest feeling that he was dropping into a deep ravine with nothing to grab hold of and no one to help him.

He turned and stalked away before he could do something really stupid and go after her again.

CHAPTER EIGHT

'THERE HAS TO be a mistake.' Harper spoke in her best, calmest voice as she looked at the clerk across the shiny marble desk. 'I booked two rooms. See?'

'Yes, madam.' The clerk had turned beet-red. 'And I can only apologise again, most sincerely, for this mistake. For some reason, the computer system took one of the rooms from your booking and allocated it to another guest.'

'Well, we require two rooms,' she said, refusing to think about the man standing behind her, listening to this conversation. 'One for Mr da Rocha and one for me.'

'I understand, madam, and again,] I apologise, but we have only the one room available. I can make some calls to different hotels in the city, to see if there is availability, but with the festival Prague is very heavily booked.'

She ground her teeth together. 'Festival?'

'Prague Majales,' he said with a nod. 'I can thoroughly recommend you walk through the town to enjoy it.'

'I'm not really in a festival mood,' Harper said wearily.

'I am sorry.' The clerk's gaze encompassed Harper and Salvador. 'Allow me to make a suggestion.'

'Go right ahead.' Salvador's voice dripped with ice and Harper shivered. She hadn't dared look at him since 'Room Gate' had begun, but now she lifted a gaze and saw an expression that would have turned a dragon to stone.

'The concierge will take your bags to the available room. Go make yourselves comfortable while I arrange some refreshments, with the hotel's compliments. In the meantime, I will endeavour to find a solution—at our expense—in a nearby hotel. Will this be acceptable?'

'It doesn't sound like there's much more you can do,' Harper muttered.

'Thank you, madam, sir.' The clerk either missed the tone or chose to ignore it, handing two key cards across the counter with a cheery smile. 'Enjoy your stay in Prague!'

Harper glared at him before turning away, her worst nightmares unfolding. 'There has to be another room. As soon as he finds it, I'll go.'

Salvador sent her a look that was both weary and, for some reason, bemused. 'Ask yourself if it sounded as though he was going to break a sweat trying to find something else for us,' Salvador commented, and when Harper looked over her shoulder she saw the clerk had already moved on to the next guest, busily drawing lines on a map of Prague.

She turned back to Salvador and her mood deteriorated. 'This isn't funny.'

He sobered. 'I know.'

Mollified, she moved to the lift, waiting as far away from Salvador as she could. The lift took a few minutes to arrive and, by the time it did, she and Salvador had been joined by six or seven other people who crowded in with them, pushing them together at the back of the lift. Harper stood like a stone, completely still.

At one point, Salvador's hand brushed hers and she almost jumped out of her skin, jerking into the woman beside her, who gave Harper a look of irritation. Harper stayed where she was anyway, close to the woman's shoulder, rather than risk another incendiary touch with Salvador.

For all she felt like one touch could light her bones on fire, she just had to remember the way he'd pushed her away in Venice and her desire was extinguished. She wasn't going to be made a fool of. She'd let Peter do that to her, and Harper wasn't going to make that mistake again.

'This is us,' Salvador said when the lift reached the eighth floor. He waited for Harper to step through the other guests, then followed. She looked up and down the hallway, picked the right direction then strode off, a step in front of him, determined to keep things business-like. In all likelihood, the room would be more than large enough to accommodate them both comfortably, as her rooms in Greece and Italy had been. This was a storm in a teacup. Far from ideal, but also not the end of the world.

She swiped the key card, pushed open the door and groaned.

The room was a decent enough size, she supposed, as befitted a hotel of this standard, but there was only one bed in the middle of the room—albeit a king. There wasn't even a sofa she could crawl onto, just two arm chairs near a window that overlooked the ancient city, with the afternoon sun making the wide, curving river sparkle. Oh, well. She could sleep in a chair.

'It will be fine,' Salvador said through gritted teeth. 'Absolutely fine. If you'll excuse me, I'm going to take a shower.'

A shower? She frowned. She supposed they'd been travelling for a few hours, but since when…? Unless he meant a cold shower? She pressed a hand to her forehead, trying to get rid of the idea of Salvador in the hotel bathroom washing away his desire for her— as if he wanted her *that* much. But…she did. She felt an overwhelming need for him despite their fight, despite everything. So what if he felt it too? And he was determined to fight it, even if that meant enduring icy showers?

She'd never know for sure, and it wasn't her place to know. Harper had a mountain of work to catch up on so, rather than imagine Salvador lathering his body in the shower, hot or cold, she opened her laptop and began to read emails. She flicked various ones to Salvador or the appropriate staff member, until she got through at least twenty of the things, then went over the financial reports he'd sent across for Harper to check.

This was the kind of work she loved—meticulous, complicated and important. She lost herself in concentration, so didn't hear the door to the bathroom open-

ing until, a moment later, Salvador strolled across the
room to the window dressed in only a low-slung towel,
and the movement caught her eye. The sight of him ar-
rested her gaze, making it impossible to look back at
her screen.

'Our suitcases aren't here yet,' he said simply, but
there was nothing simple about it, and his voice showed
his displeasure.

Her tongue tingled with an unwelcome inclination
to lick the last remaining water droplets from his toned
body. She scowled instead.

'This hotel isn't really up to the same standard as
the others, is it?'

'It's got the most potential,' he said with a lift of his
shoulders that did nothing to help Harper's overheated
mind for two reasons. His muscled chest shifted, his
shoulders, biceps—everything—gleaming from the
shower, but it also put the towel in grave peril. She
wasn't sure how good he was with knots—he didn't
seem like Boy Scout material—so she wasn't sure how
securely he'd anchored the towel in place. She suspected
a few more shrugs and it might drop.

Holy crap.

'This is going to be fine,' he muttered.

Harper closed the lid of her laptop with a snap. 'I'll
go back down to Reception and see if there's any news
on a room. And then I'll work from the foyer.' She
stood, conscious of how close they were in this room,
breathing the same air, always within touching distance. Her eyes swept shut because this was *not* going
to be fine.

Salvador was a trillionaire. Surely he could *pay* someone to vacate their room?

'We have a meeting at three.'

'I'll sort this out,' she said with a small nod, but her voice was soft, lacking confidence, because the desk clerk had seemed pretty adamant first time round.

He didn't argue. Harper collected her work bag and key card then slid from the room, breathing out when she reached the hallway. As the lift doors opened, the concierge arrived with their suitcases.

With a groan, she stepped into the lift and jabbed her finger against the button, waiting desperately to be whisked away to something more like normality.

At a quarter to three, Harper returned to the room, which she couldn't think of as 'theirs', because that implied too much and it hurt to imagine it. Salvador was standing looking out of the window, so for a moment she had a view of his back, strong and confident, and his powerful body, before he turned, hands in pockets, and offered a tight smile.

She volleyed back something similar. Awkward silence fell.

'I presume you weren't able to find another room?'

'No.' Her lips pulled to the side. 'Anything within a two-mile radius is booked up for the festival. I'm sorry,' she felt obliged to say.

'It was their error. There's nothing you could have done to prevent it.'

But frustration gnawed at her. 'I find it hard to imagine this happening to Amanda,' she said with a small shift of her shoulders, closing the door behind her reluctantly, because it boxed them into this tiny space. She stayed where she was, in the small entrance foyer, because it was as physically far from Salvador as she could get.

'It's beyond your control. Don't worry about it. It's one night. I'm sure we'll survive.'

Was he?

She nodded unevenly, placing her laptop bag back on the bed. 'We're meeting on the roof terrace,' she reminded him.

Salvador's nod was thoughtful; Harper's heart stammered. She had to find a way to get through this. 'Excuse me.' She bolted left, into the bathroom, slamming the door and flicking on the taps so she could wash her hands with ice-cold water and stop panicking. This was going to be a disaster.

Hold on to your anger, she thought. *Remember everything that's happened between the two of you. Remember Peter. Your dad. All the men who've let you down. Don't let Salvador have that power over you!*

Her head hurt. She reached for a glass, filled it with some water from a bottle and drained it, then took in her reflection.

It had been a long day and she was a mess. Using her fingers, she combed her hair over one shoulder and pinched her cheeks, but that was the best she could do without her cosmetics, still stowed in a bag in the hotel room.

A moment later, she emerged, eyes not meeting Salvador's as she reached for her handbag and removed her lipstick, moving to the mirror above the desk and carefully applying a fresh coat. It was amazing what a difference it made. She clicked the lid back in place, turned to locate her bag and found Salvador staring at her, a fulminating frown on his handsome features that spiked her blood pressure all over again. She stared and couldn't move. It was as though she was trapped by his gaze.

'We should go,' he said finally, voice hoarse.

She nodded, but neither of them moved. It took her a moment to galvanise herself against the waves of awareness bouncing off the walls.

'I'm ready.'

Neither moved. Salvador was backlit by the afternoon sun, and he looked god-like in stature, glowing with gold. She frowned as her feet finally stepped, but in the wrong direction, towards him, across the carpet. She stopped, feeling like an idiot. He was like a gravitational well; she found it almost impossible to pull away from him.

'This isn't a big deal.'

She frowned, not understanding what he meant.

'It's just one night.'

'Oh.' She nodded, turning to look at the bed, swallowing.

'I'll take the floor.'

'Don't be stupid, Mr da Rocha. The bed is more than big enough for both of us. We can be adult about this.'

His expression showed cynicism and a healthy degree of doubt on that score.

'Nothing's going to happen,' Harper repeated.

'Are you trying to convince me or yourself?'

She grimaced. 'Nothing's going to happen.' Her heart stitched strangely. 'We really should go. Now.'

It felt as though the building were on fire. She had to escape. Grabbing her bag, she turned and finally moved in the right direction: towards the door, out of the room and into a space that wasn't completely over-powered by Salvador.

She checked her watch again, frowning. The meeting had gone on longer than she'd anticipated. The allotted two hours had bled towards three, the manager prone to waffling and wanting to apologise again and again for the mix up with rooms—which had worn thin after the first time, let alone after at least ten attempts at ex-plaining the problem with their computer system.

Salvador, who clearly didn't suffer fools gladly, had been in no mood to tolerate the excuses.

As time passed, Harper knew she'd have to excuse herself: something she hated doing because it seemed inattentive and unprofessional but she was due to call her mother soon and there was no way she could delay.

As the manager moved towards the banquet rooms to show off the new parquetry, Harper reached out, touching Salvador's arm lightly to arrest his attention. It worked a little too well. He stopped as though he'd been electrified so she quickly dropped her hand.

She felt nervous! Harper, who'd tamed Goliaths for breakfast, was terrified of disappointing this man, of having him think badly of her. She ground her teeth, irritated by her own weakness, refusing to give into it. This was about her mother, and there was nothing that would come between Harper and her commitments there.

'I have a personal matter to attend to,' she said stiltedly. 'I have to go.'

'Go?' He frowned. 'Is this about the room?'

'What? No. I don't mean "go", as in leave Prague.' She shook her head. 'I have to go upstairs to the room. To make a call.' Her stomach twisted. 'It's important.'

He nodded thoughtfully. 'Your thirty minutes?'

She expelled a soft breath. 'It's prearranged. I can't reschedule it at this late notice. I'm sorry.'

'Don't apologise. Meet me in the bar afterwards to discuss the meeting.' His eyes flicked to the manager, who was waiting by an open door. 'I'll be done by then.'

Harper's smile was automatic. She could see that Salvador was growing impatient, and she suspected he was about to rapidly draw this tour to a close, but she couldn't stick around to enjoy watching that. Her mum was waiting.

He was more than tempted to go up to their room. Curious as all hell, in fact, to know just what she did in these thirty minutes. He now knew that it was a scheduled thing with another party, and it couldn't easily be rescheduled, but beyond that he was in the dark—not a place Salvador da Rocha generally liked to be.

He sipped his coffee, eyes fixed on the door of the bar, waiting, watchful, his whole body tense and on alert in a state of adrenaline preparing to flow.

She walked in about fifteen minutes past the time

her half-hour appointment would have ended, and something clutched in his gut low and fierce, a taste filling his mouth that he couldn't explain. Beneath the table, his hands formed balls on his thighs and his eyes clung to her as she looked around the bar, lips pressed together, eyes hooded, figure hidden in a boxy linen dress.

But he'd seen her. He'd touched her. It didn't matter what she wore; he saw her as she'd been in his office and he yearned for her.

Fire spread through his veins as he remembered the way it had felt to kiss her in Greece. The way her body had been so soft and pliant against him, her slender curves addictive, so he'd wanted to strip her naked right then and there and take her.

It had been a tempest, a storm, a raging desire, and he'd thanked whatever powers there meant that he'd been able to bring it to a close. But he was only a man, a mortal, and resisting Harper would take a superhuman effort, more strength than he possessed.

He closed his eyes for a moment and thought of Anna-Maria, thought of their baby, thought of the pain that had come from opening his heart, from opening *himself*, and he knew he couldn't weaken with Harper.

But then she looked in his direction. Their eyes met and he was sinking, without control, without consent, deep into that abyss again…but now he was no longer sure he wanted to escape.

He stood as she approached the table, the old-fashioned courtesy somehow in keeping with his character. Her heart did a funny little pop. She hovered at the seat opposite without taking it.

'How was your appointment?' he asked casually, too casually. She understood the curiosity he felt. It was natural.

Harper hesitated. She never spoke about her mother, especially not to colleagues. Revealing the vulnerability made her feel weak, or as though people might treat her differently. She liked to be seen as strong and in charge. But Salvador's voice, his eyes, everything about him, made her want to tell him the truth.

'It went well,' she said eventually, a little unevenly. The truth was, it hadn't gone well. Her mother had barely been lucid. Those days were the hardest. Harper offered a tight smile and then belatedly folded herself into the seat opposite. A waiter appeared brandishing a drinks menu. Harper ordered a coffee, taking her lead from Salvador. This was business, not a date, despite the convivial setting. 'How was the rest of your meeting?' she asked, pulling her laptop from her bag. 'Did you like the parquetry?'

He laughed, and she sat bolt-upright, the sound as welcome now as it had been the first time she'd heard it.

'Excellent parquetry,' he confirmed. 'Definitely worth buying the hotel for.'

'If not their reservation system.'

'That I could do without.'

'If these hotels are all part of the same chain, why aren't their systems the same?'

'They've been bought over the years and slowly homogenised, but this was the last to be acquired, and therefore the last to be modernised.'

'So that's a job for you.'

He dipped his head.

'Are you going to buy them?'

He scanned her face. 'What do you think I should do?'

Harper considered that, her pulse racing. 'I think you should.'

'Why? Two of them run at a loss.'

'That's true,' she agreed, leaning forward, all of the tension forgotten as she warmed to her theme, excited to have a chance to say what she'd been thinking for days when she hadn't been thinking obsessively about Salvador. 'But there's a huge amount of wastage. I checked their linen costs, for example, and they're astronomical. They're still running on a policy of laundering all towels and sheets daily. Most hotels, as a concession to the environment, offer guests incentives to reuse towels and skip housekeeping services.'

His eyes narrowed, and he remained very still, but Harper didn't notice. She was too enlivened by the chance to share what she'd been looking at.

'I ran the figures,' she continued. 'You'd save twelve per cent of operating costs if you implemented a similar scheme. That's in comparison to competing hotels in the same cities,' she explained.

'What else?'

'Food and beverage. All of the hotels offer round-the-clock room service, but between eleven at night and, say, six in the morning, it's running at a huge loss.'

'They're five-star hotels. Guests expect to be catered to at any time of day.'

'That's true,' she agreed eagerly. 'But again, I checked. There are six items that are most commonly ordered between those hours. The kitchen could run a limited overnight menu, as lots of hotels do, and cut overnight staffing costs by more than half, without affecting guest satisfaction. A more substantial minibar offering would also meet late-night cravings, and as you know the profit margin for minibars is huge.'

'You enjoy this.' It was a statement, not a question.

'Yes.' It was like being jolted out of a dream. Harper blinked and looked around them, realising that she was talking to one of the most successful businessmen in the world, as if he wouldn't already know how to maximise profits. 'Anyway,' she said with a shrug. 'I'm sure I'm not telling you anything you haven't already realised.'

He was silent, watchful, and she was glad when her coffee arrived because it gave her something to do with her hands. Salvador turned to the waiter. 'We'll take a couple of menus, thanks.'

'Yes, sir.'

'Oh.' Harper's cheeks flushed. 'I'm not— I don't think—'

'I'm hungry,' he said with a steely look in his eyes. 'You must be as well. Besides, it makes sense to sample the hotel food.'

But consternation flooded Harper. She couldn't do this. It was all too complicated, with too many layers of competing wants, needs and dangers.

'I—'

'It's just dinner.'

'But it's not,' she said with an exasperated shake of her head. 'Let's at least call a spade a spade.'

'We've eaten together before.'

'That was before.'

'Before what?'

'Greece.'

His expression barely shifted but she saw the tightness around his eyes and felt the air between them hum. The waiter appeared with menus, but even that didn't break the tension.

'Thank you,' Harper murmured, barely lifting her eyes from Salvador's face.

When they were alone again, he put his hand on the table top, extending his fingers then squeezing them into a fist before relaxing them again. He looked as though he wanted to say something, or maybe as though he desperately didn't, so she waited, wondering, and finally he spoke.

'My wife died a year ago,' he said quietly. 'But I can't stop feeling guilty for wanting you like this.' It was so honest—so wrenchingly honest. She felt his grief and wanted to wrap her arms around him, to tell him everything would be okay, even when she didn't know if it would be. She settled for reaching over and putting her hand on his in a spontaneous gesture of comfort. It felt so important, so right.

'I'm very sorry for your loss, Mr da Rocha.'

He lifted a single dark brow.

'Salvador,' she supplied with a frown. Then, because

she was a glutton for punishment, 'You must have loved her very much.'

'I'd known her for a long time,' he said after a pause. 'We were friends,= as children. She moved to Italy as a teenager, but we wrote to each other.'

She nodded slowly. And then they'd fallen in love. It was so…romantic. Jealousy was unmistakable. She wished she didn't feel it, but it was clawing through her.

Salvador stared directly at her, almost through her. Harper shivered. There was so much emotion, so much pain, in the man. She didn't know what to say or how to comfort him, except by sharing some of her own pain to show that he wasn't completely alone.

'My mother is in a nursing home,' she said slowly, the words not ones she formed often. When was the last time she'd spoken about this to anyone besides Amanda?

'She had a stroke seven years ago. It left her partially paralysed. Then, two years after that, a series of strokes left her with brain damage.' Harper's voice quivered a little. She couldn't meet Salvador's eyes. 'Her condition is unpredictable.' She lifted her shoulders. 'Some days, she seems to recognise my voice, to know who I am. Other times, like today, there are no lights on.'

Harper shook her head. 'My mother was one of the most fiercely intelligent women you've ever met. Funny, charismatic and so utterly beautiful. She was like a fairy or a ballerina, something out of a story book. I used to love watching her get ready for shows—she was an actress,' Harper explained. 'I grew up back stage in the theatres, watching her perform.' A cloud crossed her features then, darkening the lights from within her own eyes. 'It's very difficult to see her like this.'

'You call her every day?' he prompted.

She nodded, unable to speak.

'For thirty minutes?'

Harper swallowed. 'I read to her. Scripts, books she used to love…anything. I just want to offer her some comfort, Salvador. Some hint of the woman she used to be.'

'What's her prognosis?'

She appreciated the question, because it was practical and it gave her a chance to blink away her tears and focus on the black-and-white medical situation. 'No one knows. She could live for decades like this, with the right care.'

His eyes honed in on hers. 'But that care is expensive.'

'Yes.' Her smile was wistful. 'Very.'

'You pay for it? There's no husband—insurance?'

'No and no.'

'Your father?'

She shook her head. 'Long gone. And, while mum was pretty successful, she was diagnosed with diabetes a little while after I was born, and it cost a fortune to buy her insulin and other meds, so her savings are pretty non-existent.' Harper grimaced. 'She managed to put a little away for me, over the years. For college.'

Salvador watched without speaking.

'Then she had her stroke and the hospital bills mounted up…'

'You used your tuition savings for hospital fees?'

She nodded. 'Of course.' There was determined pride in that answer, and she tilted her chin at him with a hint of defiance. 'What else could I have done?'

'Nothing,' he agreed after a pause, but the admiration was difficult to miss. 'What did you intend to study?'

'Pre-law.' Another pause, as she took a moment to wonder why she was being so forthcoming. But, much like their physical connection, it was difficult for Harper to control this. There was magic weaving around them, making her want to confide in Salvador, almost to bare her soul to him.

'Had you applied anywhere?'

Heat flushed her cheeks as she nodded.

'And been accepted?'

She nodded again.

'Where?'

'Georgetown. I got a scholarship place, but I couldn't leave mum.'

Sympathy softened Salvador's eyes and he flipped his hand to capture hers, the hand she hadn't realised she was still holding, his eyes locked on Harper's, a challenge in their depths.

'Have you thought about applying for a position through the company?'

She shook her head. 'I missed my opportunity, Salvador. I dealt with that a long time ago. This is what I do now, and I'm very, very good at it.'

He linked their fingers, and her pulse went haywire. What was he doing? Did he know how this was making her feel? Her stomach was in knots, looping like crazy.

'Anyway,' she said awkwardly. 'I don't know why I

told you all that. I guess I suppose I just wanted you to know that… I understand…grief and loss and life not turning out how you wanted it to.'

'Thank you.'

It was a funny thing to say and she smiled softly, then went to pull her hand away, but he didn't release his grip and Harper didn't fight. She surrendered to the contact, sighing a little, inching forward in her seat so their knees brushed beneath the table. Neither moved away.

The waiter came to take their orders. Harper's heart was in her throat. Everything felt strange and uncertain, but the same hand at her back that seemed like that of fate or something more was pushing her now, so she heard herself say in a voice that was croaky and uneven, 'I…would be happy to eat in the room.'

Salvador's eyes flared. 'To trial room service?' he said quietly, one side of his lips lifting in a half-smile. 'That does make sense.'

'Yes,' she agreed, because it absolutely did.

CHAPTER NINE

HE DROPPED HER hand when they stood and left the hotel bar, but once they were in the lift their hands brushed and his fingers sought hers lightly…seeking reassurance? Or looking to give it to her, more likely, because Salvador wasn't the kind of man who'd need reassurance.

Except Harper felt the magnitude of this.

Whatever 'this' was.

It was new territory for both of them, and she barely wanted to exhale in case the sound of her breath knocked them off-course. Now it wasn't enough to consider Salvador's concerns, but her own as well, because she'd been running for years from the mistake with Peter, and she didn't want to make another one. She worked for Salvador, not just for this fortnight but back in Chicago, and she needed to be sure this wouldn't become public knowledge. She needed to know it wouldn't change anything for her.

'Salvador?' She turned to face him and her stomach dropped to her toes because he was so devastatingly beautiful. When she looked at him, nothing mattered.

She'd lose her job. She'd quit. She'd sacrifice almost anything for this one night with him.

But there was her mother to consider, and everything she'd worked for.

'You were right, the other day,' she whispered. The lift doors pinged open and another couple stepped in. Harper went to pull her hand free but again Salvador held onto it, his eyes meeting hers, charged with an electrical current. She sucked in a breath, tipping towards something, unable to think clearly.

She didn't speak until they reached their floor and they stepped into the corridor, walking side by side towards the room. Salvador swiped his key, the door clicked open and Harper stepped inside, her pulse raging in her eardrums.

'What was I right about?' he asked, unbuttoning his shirt at the collar to reveal his neck. She tried to move her mouth but found it almost impossible.

She pulled her hair over one shoulder, toying with the ends. 'My last job, I was involved with someone. My boss.' She dropped her hands in front of her, wringing her fingers together. 'It was a very, very bad decision.' She blinked into his eyes. It felt a little like looking at a solar eclipse.

He moved closer, lifting her chin. 'What happened with him?'

She chewed on her lower lip. She didn't really want to bring Peter into this situation. He was part of her past, a part she didn't like to think about often, except as to the lessons she'd learned from it all. 'It was a stupid mistake.'

He waited silently.

'We spent a lot of time together. I liked him. He asked me out on a date, and I knew I should have said no, but it was all so hard—stuff with Mum—and I was lonely. I agreed, reluctantly at first. But it was so good to have someone to talk to, even though, looking back, he did most of the talking.' She shrugged. 'I liked not being alone.' Her voice cracked. 'But it was all a lie. I was totally naïve and inexperienced, Salvador.' She groaned. 'I wish I'd been able to see what kind of man he was—or that not wanting to be alone wasn't a good enough reason to sleep with him.'

'When you say totally inexperienced, do you mean that literally?'

Harper's throat shifted as she swallowed, suddenly self-conscious. 'Caring for Mum, the worry, it took all my time. I never had a chance to meet anyone.'

Salvador's expression changed slightly. 'Did he know?'

'That he'd be my first? Yes. He got off on it, I'm pretty sure. If only I'd known he was married,' she said witheringly. 'He promised me the world but all the while he was going home to his pregnant wife every night.' Bitterness tinged her words. 'Thank God I found out about her after just a few weeks. I can't bear to think how long he would have strung me along for.'

Salvador cursed, wrapping his arms around her waist, drawing her against his body. 'Any man who can behave like that isn't worth an ounce of your time.' He ran his thumb over the base of her spine. 'Did he fire you?'

'God, no, I quit. The same afternoon I found out about his wife. I couldn't bear to be in the same building as him, let alone the same office. I hated him, Salvador. Whatever my feelings had been beforehand, they were unmistakably filled with hatred then.'

'Good. I'm glad. And now?'

'I still hate him,' she admitted. 'Not with quite the same passion, but that's only because I realise he's probably a serial offender. He lied too easily…it was all too smooth. There's no way I was his first affair.'

'More than likely.'

'After that, I swore I'd never get involved with someone I worked with. Come to think of it, I didn't really see me getting involved with anyone.'

He nodded slowly. 'We don't have to do this.'

'Don't we?' she prompted with a small sound, something like a sob, shaking her head a little, because this felt as inevitable to Harper now as it had back on the island that first day in their shared office space.

'I don't want to hurt you, Harper. I don't want to be like him.'

She loved hearing him say her name, even in a sentence that was so full of doubt and concern.

'You won't and you're not. You never could be.' She knew that deep in her heart.

'I haven't slept with a woman in a long time. Years.' The revelation caught her off-guard. She knew he'd been celibate since his wife had passed, but before that? He lifted a hand to her cheek, running his thumb over the soft flesh there. 'I don't want you to read more into this than is there. I don't want to make you promises. I don't want you to think—'

'I don't think anything,' she said quietly.

'Having sex with you is more than I thought I'd let happen. It can't go beyond this.'

She ignored the strange sensation in the middle of her chest, letting his words permeate her soul. He was being honest—something Peter had never had the courage to do. Salvador wasn't pretending this was a prelude to any great future. It was just sex.

'I don't—I can't make sense of what's happening between us,' she said after a beat, being completely honest. 'But I know I'll always regret it if I walk away before letting this play out. Does that make sense?'

He groaned. 'I hate that I can't control this.' Their eyes met and held. 'But, hell, I don't want to control it either. Does that make sense?'

All the sense in the world. She blinked up at him, nodding once, and then he kissed her, slowly, tentatively. It was as if he were signing on the dotted line, a deal with the devil, making a pact that he knew he'd regret later but couldn't resist in this moment. And then, as she kissed him back, any pretence of being gentle was thrown by the wayside, the kiss becoming urgent, desperate, so animalistic and wild, his big, strong body practically swallowing hers as he wrapped his arms around her and pulled her to his chest. His fast-beating heart hammered against hers, which beat with the same frantic answering rhythm, pounding against her ribs frantically and with force.

His hands found the hem of her dress, lifting it fast

as though he couldn't wait to remove it, as though he needed to see her naked more than he'd ever needed anything. She sucked in a breath, but it was hard because he was kissing her, and she didn't want to break that contact. They were a tangle of tongues and lips, arms, hands and legs, moving with the same purpose, desperate to connect flesh to flesh, to feel and explore.

The dam had burst, the power of a thousand rivers exploding into the room as they stumbled back to the bed, clothes dropping, hands searching, touching, needing, wanting, kissing. His body was over hers, naked except for his boxer shorts, and her hands roamed his back, her nails dragging over his bronzed skin, her lips finding his collar bone, kissing him, tasting him, drowning in a wave of desire, desperate to be fulfilled.

His arousal was so hard against her, reminding her of his hunger, of his need, of the fact he hadn't been with a woman in years. Suddenly, the rush of knowing that she'd be his first filled her with something other than desire and adrenaline, with something more, despite the limitations of what they were doing. And yet, how could she not read a little something into this? It wasn't that either of them wanted a relationship, but that didn't make this meaningless.

Everything had meaning and the fact they'd been thrown together and had chosen one another was shaping parts of her she'd forgotten existed.

She'd only ever been with Peter, and the sex had been okay. Not earth-shattering, not amazing, but pleasant enough most of the time. But this was different. From the first moment she'd met Salvador, there'd been a chemistry there that had threatened to burn Harper alive.

His hand guided her legs apart and she jumped, so unused to being touched there she didn't know how to respond except to cry out. His eyes flew to hers, checking on her, making sure she was okay, and then he kissed her once more, making it impossible to think of anything but this connection, the rightness of what they shared.

'Salvador.' She bit down on her lip, unsure what she wanted to say, just knowing this was more perfect than she could express. 'I need—'

'I know.' His hand moved between her legs, touching her there, feeling her moist core, and she bucked against his hand, so drenched with desire she was already at a precipice. Pulling up onto his elbow, he watched her, his hand moving slowly at first, enquiring, as his eyes probed her face—reading her, watching what made her moan, what drove her wild, getting to know her until, within minutes, he was playing her body so expertly it was as though he'd been practising for this his whole life.

She couldn't control herself. Pleasure exploded through her, her release swift and complete. She wrapped her legs around him and pushed up, needing to kiss him to somehow process the pleasure she was feeling, to wean herself off the high, to cope with the waves that were ravaging her body and shocking her with their intensity.

If she stopped and thought about it, the last few days had been like a wild kind of foreplay. She'd wanted him from almost the first moment they'd met, and bit by bit they'd danced around the subject, probing, promising, even while insisting it wasn't what either of them wanted. And now there was this, the most catastrophic explosion of desire she'd ever known—and it was only just beginning.

Her hands ran down his torso, feeling the ridges of his abdomen, the muscled form, until she brushed the thatch of hair at the base of his arousal and he stilled. She felt his body tremble and, emboldened, moved her hands to clasp his length, squeezing him gently so she heard that sound she'd come to love: the sharp hiss of breath that told her he was at a tipping point.

'Harper.' Her name was a warning, one she didn't heed.

His tip had a hint of pearly liquid already and power soared through her, the knowledge that she'd driven him to this point, that he wanted her so badly.

'Stop.' He groaned, even as he moved within her grip, encouraging her to keep going. 'I'm going to come if you keep touching me like that.'

'Is that a bad thing?' She purred.

'I want to feel you.'

Her heart stammered. 'I want that too.'

He moved then, pulling out of her grip, moving closer and then freezing, pulling up to stare into her eyes, his skin pale beneath his swarthy complexion.

'What?' Her heart sank. *Please, please, don't put an end to this,* she silently pleaded.

'I don't have any condoms.'

The words didn't quite make sense to Harper at first; she was in such a fog of sexual pleasure and euphoria.

'What?'

'Nothing. I have nothing. Why would I?' he said with a gruff laugh that was lacking amusement. 'This was definitely not on my radar.'

She swore. 'I don't either. Same reason.'

They stared at each other, totally bemused and utterly frustrated. He groaned, dropping his head to her shoulder, his breath rough. Harper's pulse was thready, her need growing by the second. She moved her hands back to his length, feeling him convulse, feeling his strength and his power. She desperately wanted to feel him inside her, but at the same time she wanted to drive him to the point of explosion with her hands, because she could do that right now, she could make him feel a thousand things.

'Don't fight me,' she instructed, moving one hand and then the other over his tip, down his length, feeling him, worshiping him. His head stayed where it was in the crook of her neck, his desperation at fever pitch, his breath so warm against her skin, his need so absolute that he surrendered to this finally, to her, to whatever they were to each other.

His breath grew rushed, his voice deep, then he groaned, swore and pulled up to stare at her, but she didn't release him. She moved her hands faster, until he was coming over her bare chest and she was crying out, because it was so illicit and animalistic, so completely full of abandon, that it was the sexiest thing she'd ever felt.

He dropped his head to hers, kissing her, breathing her in, the smell of him in the air, of pleasure and satisfaction, and then he pulled up, staring at her as if he needed to commit this exact image to memory, for all time.

She wasn't self-conscious. Not even a little. She felt exultant, euphoric, and the way he was looking at her only cemented that.

'Come with me.' He reached for her and she put her hands in his, allowing him to pull her to sitting then scoop her up and carry her, cradled against his chest, into the bathroom. It wasn't overly large, but it accommodated both of them easily enough, so he carried her into the shower cubicle and placed her onto the tiled floor, flicking the switches and waiting until warm water began to flow. He stared at her again, drinking her in, studying her, and then shook his head with an expression that was almost impossible to fathom.

'Will you promise me to stay here?'

Something lodged in her throat. 'Where are you going?'

'To find a pharmacy. Or a vending machine. Any kind of prophylactic. I will ask at the bar if I have to,' he ground out, so she laughed.

'I'm sure there'll be a shop somewhere.'

'Stay here.' He hesitated for the briefest moment then leaned in, kissing her hard and fast before pulling away and turning his back. He left the bathroom without closing the door, so a moment later she caught a glimpse of him stalking past, fully dressed and looking more or less completely normal. But Harper had seen him lose

his mind and now, she overlaid his passion, his powerful, sensual nature, with the visage he showed to the
world and she knew there was so much more to him,
so much he would show her.

She washed herself slowly, luxuriating in the way
her body was so sensitive all over, in the way it felt to
brush a loofah over her breasts, her thighs, her stomach.
She groaned as her hand came close to her sex and she
remembered how easily he'd undone her, how skilfully
he'd mastered her body, and she tilted her head back
and pressed it against the tiles as memories overcame
her. She stood there for a long time, the water deluging
her, reaching for the taps just as the front door opened
and Salvador returned.

Her heart fluttered and her insides squeezed. He
lifted a brown paper bag, a half-grin making his face
so wonderfully sexy that she smiled back fully, properly. She stepped out of the shower as he moved into
the bathroom, reaching for a bath sheet, wrapping her
in the fluffy fabric and towelling her down slowly from
her very wet hair to her shoulders, her breasts, her abdomen, kneeling in front of her to dry between her
legs, her calves, her ankles and her feet. She submitted
to it, but it was a form of torture to feel him so close
yet not have him buried inside her yet—more foreplay
after days and days of wanting but knowing him to be
off-limits.

She shivered, so he lifted his face from where he
knelt. 'Cold?'

She shook her head.

His smile was knowing, but Harper couldn't have realised what he was about to do. Her experience was limited, and Peter had never once kissed her most intimate flesh; he'd never even shown any interest in that. But Salvador leaned forward from where he knelt, pressing his lips to her inner thigh first so she gasped, then moving to the hair at the top of her legs, parting her seam with his tongue and skilfully finding the part of her that was so receptive to his touch.

He flicked her and tasted her, sucking her, probing her until she was quivering with desire and moaning into the tiled bathroom, her frantic cries bouncing off the walls. Harper didn't care how noisy she was, though; she was barely aware of anything: time, space, place or person. She was only a conduit for euphoria now.

He gripped her hips, swivelling her at the same time he shifted his position so she was facing the mirror. It gave her something to lean against and she propped her hands on the marble counter as it became almost impossible to stand. It also gave her a perfect view of this debauched scene in the bathroom mirror—his dark head intently focussed on her femininity, her flushed cheeks, fevered eyes, pert nipples and quivering, goosebump-covered skin. She looked wanton and ravaged, and she loved it.

She moved one hand to his head, running her fingers through his hair, something bursting inside her at the joy of that—at the freedom to touch him finally, to delight in him like this.

'Salvador...' She groaned, almost unable to bear this a moment longer. He understood. His fingers dug into her buttocks and then he sucked her flesh a little harder, flicked and she died against his mouth. Her knees were so weak she almost crumpled to the floor, so his hands at her rear became an essential part of her support. She pressed her own hand into the marble counter, crying out, almost devastated by the strength of her orgasm.

Before had been mind-blowing; this was reality-ending. She moved her hand to his shoulder and dug her nails into his flesh, as if to convey how close she was to ceasing to exist. He waited, mouth moving to the flat flesh of her belly and planting a kiss there. Then he stood, eyes hooked to hers for a moment before he lifted her once more, carrying her out of the bathroom.

She didn't protest. She really didn't think she could walk anyway.

He dumped her on the bed, staring down at her again, his breath ragged, his eyes devouring her.

'You're over-dressed,' she said simply.

He grunted his agreement. 'What are you going to do about it?'

It was a challenge and a dare, and she grinned. What was that expression—something about a goose and gander? She stood shakily, glad when he put a hand out and caught her behind the back, drawing her to him, kissing the flesh in the curve of her neck and making it impossible to think, much less act. But she needed to act, she needed to peel his clothes from his body piece by piece.

Her fingers undid the buttons, just as she had in the office that time, but now there was no fear he'd pull away, no sense that she'd gone too far. She dropped his shirt on the ground then, with eyes holding his, she knelt down in front of him, just as he'd done with her a moment ago. Her head tilted up as she undid his belt first, then his trousers, pushing them down his legs as he stepped out of them. She stayed there, looking all the way up his naked body to his eyes at first, and to the flush of his cheeks, before turning her attention to his rock-hard arousal, smiling a little as she leaned closer and tentatively ran her tongue over the tip.

He swore, the curse filling the hotel room, his hips bucking at the contact.

'Harper, no.'

'Why not?' She purred.

'You know why not. I want to feel you.'

'And you will.' She ran her tongue around his circumference. 'But first I want to taste you.'

Another curse, this one on a rough exhalation like a surrender, and then she opened her mouth and took him all the way to the back of her throat, revelling in the power of this—in the way he jerked in her mouth, in the way she could already taste him, in the way he was so incredibly big and powerful so that her insides were jumping at the prospect of accommodating him, of squeezing around his length.

She moved her mouth, wishing there was a mirror here for him to see, wishing she could watch this. There was something so incredibly sexy about feeling him in her mouth, about the way he filled her. She trembled against his body and then he caught her beneath her arms, lifting her until their eyes were almost level, his expression taut, stern, as though he was holding on for dear life.

'I want you,' he said simply. 'It's been a very long time. I can't wait any more.'

She understood. She felt a ripple of excitement as they reached for the bag in unison. He got there first, ripping it open and pulling a foil square from a box, sheathing himself quickly for someone who was out of practice.

And now, at that moment of change, of intimacy, Harper felt a rush of nervousness, because this was more than just sex. It was more to both of them because of what they'd each come through. She stared up at him but he smiled, a tight smile, showing the pain he felt at waiting, and she smiled back because she'd made her peace with this. She knew what they were and what they could never be because of how he still felt about his wife. All she wanted was to have this moment, this single night.

He kissed her at the same time as moving forward so she fell backwards on the bed with him on top of her, so heavy and strong, so hard. His thigh moved between her legs, his knee wedging her apart so his tip could press to her sex, and she whimpered, desire flushing through her body.

'Tell me if this hurts,' he ground out, and then she got why he warned her. Because, though he'd felt big in her mouth, when he began to press inside her she realised that he was really quite huge, stretching her so that she froze a moment and he did likewise, staring down at her. 'Okay?'

She nodded, because she was. Once she got used

to it, she was fine. Hungry for him, in fact hungry for more. For all of him.

'Please,' she said simply, lifting her hips, begging, inviting, needing.

He groaned as he sank all of him into her, hitched right to his base, and she cried out, the shocking feeling of how completely he possessed her overwriting everything and anything she'd thought she knew about sex. She might as well still have been a virgin. No man had ever touched her like this.

A sheen of tears filmed her eyes and she blinked furiously, desperate for him not to see or notice, not to worry that this meant something more to her than it was supposed to. It didn't. It was just such good, hot sex. She'd had no idea…

And it became even more mind-blowing once he started to move, thrusting in and out, slowly at first, letting her get used to this and him. Then finally, with all the force of his pent-up desire and long-ignored needs, he pushed into her hard and fast so her body banged against the bed and she cried out with each desperate, hungry thrust. Her own desire pushed to fever pitch, to breaking point, and she called his name into the room, dragging her nails into his back and digging in when her orgasm obliterated her soul in one fierce, agonising moment.

She could hardly breathe, barely see. She lay there, quivering, overcome, totally overpowered. Salvador watched her, satisfaction in his features, pleasure and heat, and then he began to move—with no mercy. He was enjoying this too much. Hell, so was she, and her expectations had been lowered by how long he'd been celibate.

What a fool she'd been to underestimate Salvador! He brought his A-game to whatever he did, and right now that was pleasuring Harper.

He grunted and then pulled out of her completely, pressing his hands to the bed on either side, his breath as forced as if he'd just run a marathon.

'What is it?' she asked, lifting a hand, pressing it to his chest. His heart punched her from the inside.

'Come here.' The command in his tone was as hot now as it had been the first time they'd met and he'd bossed her around. She bit down on her lip to hold back her smile and let him pull her from the bed, going with him as he moved her across the room to a mirror—of course there was a mirror in here—standing in the corner.

'I want to see this. I want you to see it.'

Standing behind her, he moved one hand to her sex and another to her breasts, playing her with the same skill as he'd shown earlier. But this time she was watching how he commanded her, how his hands moved over her, tweaking her nipples, separating her sex. At her back, she felt his arousal, wet from her own desire, nuzzled between her bottom, so on instinct alone she pressed back against him, needing everything he could give her, all that he was, needing him with a passion that she'd never known possible.

He separated her legs and, with their eyes locked in the mirror, he took her and she cried out, tilting her head back, her crown hitting his clavicle, sensations overpowering her as his hands roamed her body, tormenting her.

Finally she had to look, to see, to witness what he was doing to her. She lifted her head bravely, stared in the mirror and almost wept for how beautiful this was. There was something so right about this, about the way they came together, the way they fitted and pleasured each other, about the way they experienced desire and lust as one. Then, finally, release in lockstep, each spilling over the edge, their frantic cries in unison as they tumbled headlong into the kind of pleasure reserved for gods in books of magic and myth.

Harper wasn't sure she'd ever feel human again—she didn't know if she wanted to.

CHAPTER TEN

SALVADOR WAS COMPLETELY DISCOMBOBULATED, his body separated from his mind, from his thoughts and dreams. He frowned. There was a weight on his arm he didn't understand; his eyes searched the dim light for clues as to his whereabouts, while his body surged with a rush of something he barely recognised. And then it all came back to him.

The last few hours. The bar. Their conversation. The room. Her mouth on him. His mouth on her. His possession of her. Her reciprocation. Her total abandonment to this, as if she'd known he'd needed to feel completely animal and wild when he had sex with a woman for the first time since Anna-Maria. As if she'd known everything he needed, everything he was.

The weight on his arm was her head. He turned, looking at her, something strange twisting low in his abdomen.

Guilt.

He'd expected this. He'd known it would come, but it didn't make the pain any less compelling.

It was made even worse by the fact it wasn't all just

guilt about Anna-Maria and Sofia. There was so much more. He didn't love Harper. But if he closed his eyes and imagined loving her, imagined needing her then imagined losing her—as he had so many people in his life—he couldn't breathe. He couldn't go through that again.

And you told her that, he reminded himself forcibly. *You made it clear that last night was just about sex.* She wouldn't be weaving any dreams about a future with him. It was what it was: a one-night stand.

One night?

His body revolted in response to that. Why end it now? They'd be travelling back to the island together and she'd see out the rest of her contract, which gave them one more week. If he could make sure she understood, continued to understand, that he would never want more than the kind of passion they'd enjoyed last night, why not make the most of it? They were adults, capable of understanding the difference between lust and love.

It was as if a huge weight was being lifted off his chest. Loyalty, guilt and trauma, and the darkness of those emotions, had made him celibate, but also fear. Fear of caring for someone again, of opening himself up to them and losing them. Anna-Maria had been one of his oldest, dearest friends. He'd lost his wife but he grieved a friend and the baby they'd made together.

He never wanted to feel anything like that again.

But sex was sex—wonderful, hypnotic, drugging sex. So long as he could make sure they remembered that, they could enjoy this.

And, with that in mind, he rolled onto his side, his mouth claiming Harper's as she slept, kissing her awake. Her smile against his lips was all the reassurance he needed that she welcomed his attention, that she wanted him again. Thank God because, after the years he'd gone without, he was a starving man and she the most delicious thing he'd ever tasted.

The hotel in Prague was the least impressive but the city was undeniably Harper's favourite of the three they'd visited, and not just because of how they'd spent the night. As they traversed the bridge, side by side but not holding hands—because that would have been romantic and, whatever they were, it wasn't romantic—she paused to look over the edge, sighing a little. Ancient statues stood sentry along it. 'I would love to have seen this at night,' she said, imagining how dramatic the scenery would be when all lit up.

'We were a little busy.'

She grinned, shooting him a sidelong glance. 'No complaints here.'

'We can stay another night.' The offer was obviously made spontaneously. She saw the surprise in his eyes, but then the certainty as he nodded. 'Yes, let's stay.'

Her eyes widened. 'You're sure?'

'Why not?'

Great question. Why not? She gnawed on her lip, the hint of a misgiving forming at the back of her mind, but she couldn't make sense of it. She had no idea what could be bothering her, in fact, given how perfect last night had been, so she ignored the voice, chalking it up to indecision because everything was different and new.

'Okay. What about work?'

'We can work from the hotel.'

'From that tiny room?'

He lifted his shoulders. 'Or we can do other things.'

She laughed softly. 'Uh-uh…' She waggled her finger. 'I had fun last night, but…'

When their eyes met, it felt as though she was being speared by lightning. That strange misgiving was back.

'But,' she continued, 'I don't want any special treatment. I'm working for you, just like before. Got it?'

'I might find it a little harder to concentrate.'

She poked out her tongue. 'You'll manage.'

'I might make it a little harder for you to concentrate.'

She grinned. 'We'll see.'

Later, back in the hotel, he showed her exactly what he'd meant by that, making it almost impossible for Harper to focus on anything for longer than ten minutes between his trailing fingers, wandering lips and the fact he'd stripped down to boxer shorts alone.

'This is impossible,' she said on a laugh in the late afternoon, closing her laptop and flipping onto the bed to look at him properly.

'Yes.'

'I thought you were a workaholic.'

'I'd forgotten how much I like sex.'

Something jarred in the back of her brain, but there was a salient reminder too. She imprinted the words in her mind because she knew she'd need them later. He liked sex. Not her. Not even sex with her, though obviously he did enjoy that. But she had no reason to suspect she was any more entertaining to him than a woman picked up off the streets or in any random bar might have been. He'd been alone a long time, and she'd been there. Yes, they had chemistry, but maybe he would have felt that with any woman within a yard of his age.

This wasn't special.

She wasn't special.

'I was thinking…' he reached across her for his phone '…that we should eat out tonight.'

She frowned, her heart racing despite the direction her thoughts had just been taking. 'Oh?'

'You said you wanted to see the city.'

'Yes,' she agreed, slightly breathlessly.

He kissed her quickly. 'Then let's.'

She groaned. 'You're a terrible influence.'

He lifted a brow. 'Do you mind?'

'I'll make you a deal,' Harper said, thinking quickly, knowing that it was fundamentally important to her in the circumstances to uphold her end of the bargain. She'd come here to work and she wasn't going to let a fling with her boss derail that.

'Go on.'

'I need to finish reading this report.' She gestured to her closed up laptop. 'Let me do that and then you can have me for the night.'

'I like the sound of that.'

So did Harper, but she kept her expression stern until she had his solemn agreement. Salvador was clearly a man of his word because he dressed without speaking and then moved to the door of the hotel room.

'Where are you going?'

'Out, so you can concentrate.' He winked. 'And so I'm not tempted.'

The problem was, with Salvador gone, she was almost *more* distracted. His smell was everywhere, as was the memory of his touch and the way they'd kissed and made love. She only had to look across the room in a moment of distraction to conjure the image they'd made in the mirror and her heart was bubbling with feelings that were powerful and sort of frightening. So she focussed on her work, instinctively understanding that so much was at stake for her if she didn't remember her professionalism in the midst of all this.

Work first, Salvador second.

But Salvador *was* her work. His name, his very soul, was in every document she read, every email, every business transaction that was bursting with his confidence and *passion*. So much passion! How had she missed that? She'd thought him arrogant and rude, a total jackass, but it wasn't that at all. He was just overflowing with feelings, and he'd had no way of processing them.

Her heart panged because, in another life, Harper would have loved nothing more than to help him. To be with him as he made sense of his loss, to comfort and even love him back to life, to being able to enjoy life, but that wasn't reality. It was never going to happen—not for her, or for him. They weren't those people.

With a sigh, she re-dedicated herself to her report and managed to make it to the end. Some time before six, as she was starting to feel a little bored and lonely, the door opened and Salvador strode in carrying several good quality bags, the sort used by upscale boutiques.

'You've been busy,' she murmured with obvious curiosity.

'Yes.'

'Shopping?' It wasn't an activity she would have thought he'd enjoy.

He placed the bags at the foot of the bed and, not a moment later, there was a knock on the door. He strode towards it, opened it just long enough to retrieve a bottle of ice-cold champagne and two glasses from the hotel staff member then closed it swiftly with his foot.

'Take a look.' He gestured to the bags as his hand moved over the champagne top, after placing the glasses down to enable him to remove the foil and unfurl the cork with a muted pop as he caught it fully in his palm. A little liquid frothed over but he had the glasses ready to splash it in.

Curiosity got the better of Harper and she moved to the end of the bed, opening the closest bag and pulling out a dress of red silk all the way to the floor. Her eyes lifted to Salvador's, her expression unchanged despite the lava pouring into her veins.

'I don't know if it's your style,' she murmured, draping the dress over the end of the bed and moving to the next bag. Shoes and a clutch bag. The next contained lingerie that made her cheeks sting.

'You really have been busy.'

He lifted his shoulders. 'I found it impossible to concentrate on anything *but* you and, as you made yourself unavailable to me, this was the next best option.' He moved to the final bag. 'I enjoyed choosing these,' he said, voice gruff. 'I enjoyed, even more, imagining you wearing them.'

'And removing them?'

'That thought didn't cross my mind,' he lied badly, pulling her towards him and kissing her slowly. But it didn't matter that it was slow—the fireworks in her bloodstream exploded with all the speed of a Gulfstream jet.

Harper, who'd learned to be in control of almost all situations, felt ridiculously nervous as she surveyed her image in the hotel mirror. Salvador had gone downstairs to wait, giving her privacy and space to get ready, which she'd appreciated. As lovely as the city was, and as eager as she was to explore it, she was even keener to keep exploring Salvador. If he'd stayed in the hotel room much longer, she'd have asked him to get a refund on the dress, shoes and all and order in.

Perhaps pre-empting that, he'd showered and changed into a dark suit with a crisp blue shirt, leaving Harper to get ready, the smell of his cologne in the air making her body tingle with anticipation.

It wasn't helped by the sensation of the silk lingerie he'd chosen. It was so fine and luxurious, so incredibly soft against her body. She ran her hands over the mix of lace and fabric and wondered why she'd never bought anything like this for herself.

Because it was so sexy.

The kind of thing a man would buy for his lover.

Only, it didn't have to be. Feeling sexy wasn't just for people in relationships, or people who were having sex. She liked the way this felt. She loved it. And she loved the way it looked.

With a smile, she turned away from the mirror and removed the dress from the edge of the bed. More silky, satin-like material. The dress was a thing of beauty. It had long sleeves and wrapped around her torso, tying at the waist and falling to her ankles, so it was somehow elegant and incredibly sensual all at once. Maybe the sensuality came from knowing she was dressing for Salvador in a dress he'd chosen and would later peel off her body. It showed off her slender waist and the curves of her breasts and hips, and the long, draping sleeves meant she'd be warm enough.

The shoes were a perfect fit—how in the world had he managed that? She could barely remember her own shoe size. She felt like Cinderella, dressing for the ball.

Her eyes travelled to the mirror and her hand lifted to her hair, which she'd parted in the middle and pulled into a low bun at the back of her nape. It was a sophisticated style for a sophisticated dress and the result was breath-taking. It had become second nature for Harper to play down her looks, because more than anything she wanted to be recognised for what she was capable of. But she felt a thrill of pleasure to see herself like this, to know that Salvador had chosen this dress for her because he'd wanted to see her in it. It was sensual and somehow one of the most heart-warming things Harper had ever felt.

Turning away quickly, cheeks warm, she grabbed the essentials from her sensible leather handbag and transferred them to the sparkly clutch Salvador had bought: lipstick, phone, credit card, room key.

Feeling more and more like Cinderella, she left the room with her fingers crossed that this would be every bit as magical as Cinderella's ball. Only there'd be no falling in love with Prince Charming, she reminded herself as she approached the lift.

Much like Cinderella's expectations, this would be a one-time thing—a treat to herself, a slice out of time, before she got back to real life and her normal self.

Except, Harper wasn't sure she could slip back to normality. She wasn't the same woman she'd been in Chicago. So much had changed since then! Even having the confidence to show Salvador that she was interested had been a big step for Harper. Everything that had happened between them had changed something inside her. She'd grown and she liked how she'd changed. She felt as though a door had opened up, showing her a world in which she might have more faith in herself to reach out and grab life with both hands.

When it came to adventure, she'd never been afraid. She'd tried it all—bungee-jumping, sky-diving, rock climbing, abseiling—and she'd loved it all. The high of surfing the biggest waves in the world, with the real threat of being pummelled by the ocean, was like nothing she'd ever known.

But when it came to people, to relationships, to trust

and even love, she'd been so cautious. She'd learned to be. Seeing her mother's hurt, and then feeling that first-hand courtesy of Peter on her first foray into the world of relationships, well, had only confirmed what she'd feared all along: that hearts were made for breaking.

So maybe she still didn't want to think about love and giving her heart to anyone else, but there was a lot of middle ground between being determinedly single and getting married. Such as dating. Such as having sex. Such as dressing up and going out with the intention of meeting a guy and keeping things light and low key. It was something she'd avoided assiduously but suddenly she could see the advantage to it. She liked this. She wanted more of it.

With someone else…? A little voice in the back of her mind had her crashing back to reality. Her red lips parted in surprise and, just like that, her pleasant real-isation-bubble burst.

She was having fun *with Salvador.* She liked sleeping *with Salvador.* What if none of this was as good with anyone else?

She stepped into the lift, smiled weakly at an elderly couple already in the space and turned to face the front. Her reflection greeted her there, reminding her of how beautifully Salvador had chosen for her. She blinked away, self-conscious. This was not how she generally presented herself to the world. But Salvador made her feel…

It was Salvador, she realised with a little clutch in her heart. Maybe she hadn't changed at all, but rather Salvador had brought out qualities in her she'd never acknowledged before. Would she still feel this way in Chicago? She'd find out in a little over a week, she supposed.

Salvador had said he'd wait in the bar but he hadn't really enjoyed the experience of waiting. He was strangely energised, restless, unable to sit still properly or to focus. He had ordered a Scotch, taken a single sip then pushed it across the table and sat with one ankle crossed over the other knee, eyes on the door to the bar, just like the day before, so he'd see her the moment she walked in. Only the bar was much busier at night, filled with hotel guests, from children to people in their dotage and everyone in between milling around, laughing, drinking and talking happily. So he didn't have as clear a line to the entrance as he'd have liked. But he forced himself to sit still, to wait, watching, outwardly showing no hint of the adrenaline that was pumping his body like white water.

The door opened as a crowd moved past his table. He saw a flash of red. His gut tightened. He leaned forward, breath held. Dark hair… Yes, it was her. He drummed his fingers into his thigh impatiently. Was it her?

The crowd shifted slightly, so he saw properly and felt as though he'd been punched hard in the gut. Her beauty took his breath away, but it was more than that. It was her confidence. She held herself like a woman who *knew* she looked incredible. She looked perfect.

Her eyes skimmed the bar and, though he was staring at her, he was aware on his periphery of the way heads turned towards her. The same magnetic beauty he was appreciating was noticed by others in the bar. He stood, unfolding his body with slow intent, the action catching her eyes so their gazes locked.

Neither smiled. Electricity arced through the air. He felt it singe his fingertips, his toes, his chest. She lifted a hand to her ear, tucking an imaginary piece of hair back—was she nervous?—then began to walk towards him. The silk caressed her body like a second skin, falling like a waterfall over her hips and shimmering with each step she took so he had to hold back a groan. How the hell was he going to get through this night?

The dress had seemed like such a great idea at the time. Now he realised he'd bought himself several hours of torture.

'I borrowed your dress,' she said with an impish smile as she approached the table, and he laughed, because it was an excellent ice-breaker. The tension that had been making his head pulse dissipated. He put a hand on one of her hips and leaned forward, kissing her cheek, wondering at the strange throb in the middle of his chest.

'It looks better on you than it did on me. Keep it.'

She grinned in return.

'Would you like a drink?'

She looked around the bar, her lips twitching downwards as she considered that. He realised it wasn't a frown but just how she looked when she was in contemplation. 'It's crowded. Besides, we've seen this bar. I'd rather explore somewhere new.' She turned back to face him. 'Is that okay?'

The last little question did something strange to him.

He couldn't explain the rush of emotions he felt—vulnerability for her, to ask him that, and annoyance that she thought she had to. Was it because he was her boss? Or because she was so unsure of herself with men?

'Of course it's okay,' he responded, not sure if he did a great job of keeping the irritation from his voice.

'We can stay, if you want,' she said, brows slightly furrowed. 'I know you probably want to suss out the hotel a bit more.'

He shook his head, pulling her closer to him, knowing that there was one way he could get things back on an even keel and restore that beautiful confidence he'd seen when she'd first walked in. 'I want what you want,' he said simply. 'So just say the word.'

Her eyes ran over his face, as if she wasn't sure she could believe him, but then she smiled, so he smiled, because it was impossible not to.

'Then let's get out of here.'

His car was waiting—a limousine with a glass panel between the front and the back. It was plush and lovely, but Harper was nervous again. It wasn't being with Salvador; it was being with Salvador like *this*, on a date. And it didn't matter that they weren't in a relationship and that there was a very definite expiration date on this—tonight was still a date, with all the trimmings, and she really had no idea how to behave.

She didn't realise she was fidgeting with her fingers in her lap until he reached over and put a hand over them. The smile he offered was clearly meant to be reassuring but it only made her feel…something else. Unsettled. Uncertain.

She was overthinking this. And it was going to ruin the experience. She needed to get back in the moment, simply enjoy this one night. Relish being Cinderella, knowing that there would be no 'happily ever after' with her Prince Charming but that it could still be happy right now, happy tonight.

'Where are we going?' she asked as his hand pulled away from hers back to his own lap.

'A rooftop bar, for a drink,' he said. 'Then dinner.'

Her heart stammered and she settled back in the seat. She bit down on her lip, biting back a smile. 'That sounds perfect.'

The bar was exquisite—small, intimate and obviously exclusive. Salvador da Rocha naturally had no problem opening doors and, within a minute of arriving, they were welcomed inside and shown to a low-set table pressed against a window with views of the old city that were second to none. The bridge that had fascinated Harper, and so many millions of tourists ever year, was just across the city, so she could enjoy the vista of people promenading over it, the warm, golden lights making it seem so ancient and magical.

'Have you been to this bar before?'

He shook his head.

'How did you know it would be so nice?'

'A friend of mine owns the building. He recommended it.'

That sparked a thousand questions inside Harper.

What were his friends like? Had they supported Salvador in the last year? She knew he was reclusive, sticking mainly to the island, but had his friends come to visit? And had Salvador told whichever friend had recommended this bar about her? If so, what had he said?

She was glad when a waiter appeared with their drinks—a glass of champagne for her and a beer for Salvador. She was thirsty, her mouth dry, her body all tingly. She took a sip, the bubbles icy and enthusiastic.

'And the restaurant we're going to next?'

'Same friend.'

'He's from Prague?'

'He lives here now.'

'Did you see him at all, while you were here?'

'No.'

'Not this afternoon?'

'He's not really the kind of guy you take lingerie shopping,' Salvador pointed out with a wry half-smile.

Her nipples tingled against the silk of her bra and she reached for her champagne, taking a sip quickly. But Salvador's eyes had fallen to her breasts, to the obvious physical response, his smile not so much wry now as resigned.

Her heart leaped into her throat.

'You're not really the kind of guy I'd imagine lingerie shopping either,' she said with a lift of her shoulders.

'There's a first time for everything.'

Her heart stammered. Was that true? Was this really the first time he'd bought lingerie for a woman? Of course not. She focussed on the table between them, trying to steady her breath.

'Usually I have an assistant who can arrange all sorts of things for me,' he said with a hint of amusement in his voice. But there was something underneath it, a tension. She felt it even when he was trying so hard to cover it up. 'But that would have ruined the surprise a little.'

Of course. Amanda would ordinarily have been dispatched to buy things for his girlfriends, and then his wife. To research the best bars and restaurants in whatever city Salvador happened to be in and grease the wheels for him. But, because he was now sleeping with his assistant, he'd had to be a little innovative.

Harper felt the ground shift beneath her, the reality of what she'd allowed to happen slamming into her like a freight train all of a sudden. Everything had seemed so simple, predetermined almost, but the reality was she was walking the exact same path she'd walked with Peter.

It was different in many ways, but the same in one very important particular: she was sleeping with her boss.

The last time had been excruciating. But not because of the relationship, she reminded herself quickly. It wasn't the fact they'd been seeing each other that had caused Harper to quit without notice. It was the fact he'd drafted her into the role of mistress without so much as giving her a single clue that he was married. In fact, he'd gone out of his way to conceal it, never once mentioning the family he'd had across the river.

If she'd been so easily fooled by Peter, with whom

she'd worked closely for *months,* what might she be missing about Salvador?

'Are you okay?' He reached across, hand on hers.

'Yep, just fine,' she lied, smiling over-brightly, reaching for her drink and taking a generous gulp. 'What a lovely view,' she remarked, the words sounding close enough to genuine as she forced herself to settle back into her seat and look as though she was truly relaxed.

CHAPTER ELEVEN

BUT THE TENSION stayed with her all through their drink and as the car drove them across town to a restaurant that had so many potted plants out the front, it felt a little like walking through a jungle to get inside. Elegant jazz music played, with a pianist in the corner, and a waiter greeted them as soon as they entered. Whereas the night had started with delicious anticipation and pleasure, Harper was aware now of the risks coming at her from every angle.

'Mr da Rocha, we've been expecting you. This way, please.'

Salvador reached down and weaved their fingers together, holding her hand as he led her through the restaurant, to another 'best' table by a window that had a view of the greenery outside.

Salvador held out a seat for Harper and, as she took it, his hands brushed her shoulders, and she shivered. It felt so good to be touched by him, so right, but there was an answering darkness, knowing how temporary this was and, she had started to fear, how much more this meant to her than him—and how much more high stakes it was for her. After all, what was the worst that could happen to Salvador if anyone found out about their affair?

There'd be no consequences, no professional splash-back, no water-cooler gossip, no knowing looks when a promotion was announced. *Oh, God.*

'Your friend,' she blurted out, when they were alone.

He arched a brow. 'Which friend?'

'The one who helped you organise this.' She gestured to the restaurant. The waiter returned with menus, asking what drinks they'd like.

Harper frowned. 'Oh, um, a white wine, I suppose?'

Salvador ordered a bottle after the briefest glance at the wine list, then turned back to Harper. 'Go on?'

'When you asked him to arrange this, you didn't mention me, did you?'

He lifted a brow. 'Mention you?'

'By name.' She realised how silly it sounded, and made an exasperated noise. 'I'm sorry. I know that sounds paranoid. It's just... I just can't risk anyone ever finding out that we...'

His expression had grown very serious and grave, his eyes holding hers with an intensity that made it hard to focus.

'You think I told my friend I'd slept with my assistant?'

'Well, not Amanda,' she said with a small smile, but Salvador didn't return it. He was silent, so Harper sighed softly. 'I just thought you might have said... something. I don't know.'

'I didn't explain why I needed the information and

he didn't ask.' Salvador's nostrils flared and it was so like him, so arrogant and self-assured, that amusement rippled through her, lightening her mood.

'Okay.'

But Salvador wasn't prepared to let it go. 'Why do you ask?'

She pulled her lips to the side. 'It's just—after Peter,' she said with a shake of her head.

'People found out about the two of you?'

Heat flushed her cheeks. She hated the idea of Salvador knowing about her indiscretion and, worse, her stupidity.

'No. He made sure of that.' The words were tinged with bitterness. 'Because we worked together, he said it would be far better if we kept the relationship secret. I agreed wholeheartedly. I'd worked damned hard to get where I was and I didn't want the charge of having slept my way into the job.'

Salvador's eyes narrowed and his lips tightened, and she wondered if he found the idea of imagining her in bed with another man as unpalatable as she found it whenever the subject of his wife came up.

'You never considered reporting him to HR, though? You could have done so confidentially.'

'Believe me, there's no such thing. Besides, what would I have reported him for?' she said with a shrug. 'The relationship was consensual. He didn't pressure me. He didn't make me feel obligated to sleep with him.'

'You loved him?'

She frowned. She'd thought maybe she had, once upon a time, but since then she'd grown up and seen the relationship properly. 'I was impressed by him,' she said after a beat. 'He was very smart. I like smart.'

Salvador was quiet, his eyes difficult to read. They sipped their drinks in silence.

'And since him you've been single,' he said thoughtfully.

'Yes.'

'Why?'

She looked over his shoulder, trying to put that into words. 'I guess… I just haven't met anyone I was interested in. I work long hours. I like my job. I don't really go out anywhere like bars or clubs.'

'But you have friends?'

She nodded. 'I'm just not looking for a relationship.'

He frowned.

'Is there something wrong with that?'

'No…' He hesitated, though, so she knew he was puzzling over her circumstances and wasn't likely to let it go unless Harper gave him a little more information.

'My mum was devastated when Dad left,' she said in a low voice. 'She dated lots of guys. Lots and lots. And lots. Always looking for the man who was going to make everything better. And her heart was broken. Again and again and again. I was only a kid, but it was up to me to pick her up off the floor, to try to help her feel better. I hated—hated—how she would give these men such power over her. Like her worth was determined by whichever man she was dating at the time. It's not like I made a conscious decision to stay single, but I knew I couldn't ever live like she did. I didn't ever want to give so much of myself to another person that I risked getting lost, if that makes sense.'

'Perfectly.'

Their eyes met and the air between them crackled and hummed with mutual understanding.

'But you've been married,' she pointed out. 'So I'm sure your perspective is a little different.'

His lips pulled to one side then he drank from his wine.

'What was she like?' The question wasn't planned, but Harper didn't regret asking it. After their conversation, she felt that he'd opened a door to their past, to the spirit of total honesty.

'Anna-Maria was a wonderful person.' The words came out reluctantly. He clearly didn't want to talk about his late wife. Could she blame him? It had only been a year, or a little over. Not long enough to have healed.

'You must miss her.'

A muscle jerked in Salvador's jaw as he gripped his glass tight enough for his knuckles to show white.

'How long were you married?'

'Six months.' This time, he made it quite obvious he wasn't going to be drawn deeper into conversation.

The waiter reappeared to take their orders. Harper chose something at random, not having properly looked at the menu.

'Amanda spoke very highly of you.' Salvador changed the subject when they were alone once more. 'It seemed that she knew a lot about you.'

Harper's smile was genuine. 'She's one of my mum's oldest friends. I've known her since I was a baby—apparently. I don't remember that part, but I do remember her from when I was a girl and she'd come to visit. She'd always bring me little gifts from wherever she was working at the time. She was so glamorous, always overseas on assignment.'

Salvador nodded.

'My mum was the polar opposite—very beautiful and glamorous but a total scatterbrain. She was artistic and creative, so I never lacked for stories and fun, but sometimes dinner didn't get cooked until midnight, or not at all, and I rarely had the right school clothes.' Harper shrugged. 'Whereas Amanda was so organised. Her life seemed to run like clockwork. I was in awe of her efficiency.'

'So she's always been that way?'

'Always,' Harper confirmed with a nod. 'It was Amanda who recommended I apply for the position at da Rocha Industries in Chicago after I quit my last job. She didn't ask questions, but she understood I needed help, and put my CV forward to HR. I was so grateful to her.'

'You needn't be. Your work speaks for itself, Harper. I'm very impressed by you.'

It was just about the best compliment Harper could ever be paid.

She tucked it away into a fold of her brain for later examination and enjoyment. Some memories needed to be clung to, and this, she suspected, was one of them.

Prague was a truly beautiful city—the people, the history, the culture and the architecture. After finishing their dinner, which was sublimely delicious, Salvador and Harper walked across the Charles Street bridge—not holding hands, like the other couples doing an evening promenade, but with Salvador's hand lightly on the small of Harper's back, keeping her close, making her pulse simmer. It was somehow even more intimate and possessive, as though he wanted her welded to his side. He was hard, strong and firm and she fit there so perfectly. Heat flamed inside her body; she had enjoyed their night out but now, more than anything, she wanted to get back to the hotel, to their shared room and that perfect bed they'd enjoyed rumpling so much.

In the small hours of the morning, Salvador shifted a little onto his side so he could see Harper in the light cast by the full moon. She was asleep, sound asleep, and, oh, so beautiful. She'd been stunning tonight in that dress, with her hair, make-up and those heels, but he stared at her like this and felt something shift in his belly, something in his chest that he'd never felt before. It was an ache and a need that he shied away from, because he knew instinctively it was more than he should feel for her. That he was starting to want more than either of them had agreed to.

She was beautiful and she was fascinating, but that was even worse, because true danger lay in the kind of desire he felt—a desire that went beyond the physical.

Harper Lawson was the kind of woman a man could fall head over heels in love with.

Salvador had never been in love. Much like Harper, he'd had his own front-row seat to a cautionary tale of love and had always sought to avoid that. Things with Anna-Maria had been different. He'd loved his wife as one of his oldest friends, but that wasn't the same thing as headlong, romantic love. Their one night together wouldn't have happened if they hadn't been out together, drinking, dancing, laughing and if Salvador hadn't been so carefree with who he took to bed.

The next day, he'd woken up and remembered who Anna-Maria was to him, and wished he could have undone the last twelve hours of his life. It hadn't helped that she'd felt the opposite—that she'd loved him. He'd broken her heart that day, not knowing of course that she'd conceived their baby.

Everything with Harper, though, was different. She was sparky. So sparky that they couldn't help but surge when they were together. She was dangerous. This whole relationship was fraught with risks he couldn't define; he needed to remember that, to keep a grip on reality, to remain in control and not to hesitate to end it when the time came. It was the only thing that would make sense of all of this—to stay focussed on who he was and what he wanted, and that wasn't to get involved with a woman like Harper.

He couldn't. When he let his mind wander and imagined a world in which he opened himself up to this, to being with Harper without any idea of when—or if— it might end, he could see only the flip side. Only the darkness that came from trusting and loving, only the pain. She'd known enough of that, and so had he. Salvador knew he had to be strong for both of them.

* * *

Arriving back on Ilha do Sonhos was a strange moment for Harper. She'd committed so much of this scenery to her memory, because it was one of the most beautiful places she'd ever been, but now she saw it differently. It wasn't that the island had changed, but Harper had. She was different from the woman who'd flown out of here.

Something had shifted inside her, and a curiosity had been born that was almost insatiable. This was no longer a collection of trees and mountains leading to some of the most pristine beachfront Harper had ever seen: these were Salvador's trees and mountains, his home, his refuge, the place he'd chosen to live and love, the place where he'd known such awful loss.

To be here, to breathe the air, to see this scenery, was to place herself in his shoes and share a part of his life with him.

It was terrifying and all so *real*.

But Harper didn't want to think about that. There was one week left of her contract, one week left with Salvador, and she didn't intend to ruin it by overthinking anything.

She'd work hard—even harder than she had been doing—to prove to herself and him that nothing had changed for her professionally. And in the evenings…

Her heart rate kicked up a gear. In the evenings, she'd be his, as completely as she had been in Prague. Having opened the floodgates, there was no way to stem this tide. It was overpowering and relentless.

He landed the helicopter with expert skill, unhooked

his headset then turned to face her, a frown on his lips that she wanted to lean forward and kiss away.

'We should talk, before we go inside.'

Harper lifted a brow.

'Our relationship…' His frown deepened and he paused, weighing his next words with care. Despite the happiness Harper had just been enjoying, something inside her stilled now and she held her breath, waiting, uncertain, and hating that uncertainty. Hating that he might say something devastating, like he wanted to go back to the way things had been before. Pride wouldn't allow her to argue with him, even though that was the last thing she wanted.

'Yeah?' she pushed when he didn't speak for ages.

'Like you, I'm a private person,' he said eventually. 'I consider my personal life to my business alone.'

She waited, still not able to breathe properly.

'I would prefer the staff here not to suspect anything has changed between us.'

'Oh.' Relief surged inside Harper. 'That would be my preference too.'

His eyes scanned hers, as if looking for reassurance.

'It's not anyone else's business,' he muttered. 'But people talk, and I've had enough of that. After—' He hesitated. 'She died…' His voice cracked a little and tears formed in Harper's eyes because her heart was breaking for him. Sympathy squeezed inside her. He'd loved his wife so much. Anna-Maria must have been a very special person indeed. 'I felt as though everyone was speaking about it. About me. I did not enjoy that.'

'No,' Harper agreed softly. She reached over, putting a hand on his thigh, thrilled that she was able to do so without overthinking it, without worrying he might brush her hand away or frown. Instead, he reached down and squeezed her hand in his.

'So, we'll leave things as they were before,' he said with a nod. 'You have your room. If you agree, I can come to you there…'

'I'll think about it,' she said and then rolled her eyes, flipping her hand over and catching his. She lifted it to her lips and held it to her mouth, eyes sweeping shut a moment as she trapped this memory in the depths of her mind for later examination. It felt like the calm before the storm, the pause before they returned to something far more like normal life.

It was nothing like normal, nothing like before. She worked in the office beside Salvador's, but her every thought was of him. Even worse was knowing he was in the same boat. She only had to lift her eyes to look towards the glass that separated their offices and their eyes would meet. When she forced herself to focus for a period of time, she felt him watching her. It was electrifying and addictive.

The first day passed like some form of torture, both avoiding the other except for essential conversations pertaining to business and the hours moving slowly, oh, so slowly, until finally the day was over.

Harper stood, rubbing a hand over her neck and switching off her computer and sliding her laptop into a bag so she could do a little more in her room later. But for now she needed a break from the reality of being close to Salvador and not touching him, of wanting but knowing she couldn't have.

He was focussed on his screen when she approached his door, but the second she knocked he flicked a glance at her and her heart skipped.

'I'm done for the day, Mr da Rocha,' she said with the hint of a wink.

'Thank you, Ms Lawson.' Then, after a beat, 'Do you have dinner plans?'

She lifted a brow. 'It's a private island. Did you think I might swim to Rio to see a movie or something?'

He scowled. It was a lot of fun teasing him.

'No need to be sarcastic.'

'But it's fun,' she murmured.

'I can think of better ways to have fun.'

'Oh?'

'Later.' He grunted, returning his gaze to his screen, focussing as though his life depended on it.

Later couldn't come soon enough.

Salvador didn't keep Harper waiting long. She just had time to get back to her room and shower, to change into a pair of linen shorts and a tee shirt and he was there, with that brief knock and entrance, like the first time when he'd caught her in a state of undress.

'Hi,' she said breathlessly, moving across the floor quickly and straight into his arms.

He wrapped her in an embrace, kissing her hungrily, desperately, as though they'd been separated for weeks, not a single day. She could have sobbed for how great it felt to be right back here, in his arms, close to his fast-beating heart.

'I was thinking of going for a walk to the beach,' he said, breaking the kiss to pull away and look down at her. 'Join me?'

Her heart fluttered. It was different—more than she'd expected—and she agreed without hesitation. 'I'd like that.' Damn it, her voice sounded a little unsteady. She cleared her throat quickly and gave Salvador her best easy-going smile, as if it was no skin off her nose either way.

'Are you going to go dressed like that?' She gestured to his business shirt and trousers, so Salvador frowned.

'I suppose not.'

Harper skimmed his body. 'Need help getting changed?'

He laughed gruffly. 'I think I can manage.'

She pouted. 'But many hands make light work…' She reached for his shirt, lifting it out of his trousers just enough to be able to connect fingertips to bare flesh. She felt his skin bunch in response and a rush of power flooded her.

'You're impossible.' He kissed her on the tip of her nose. 'I'll meet you downstairs on the terrace.'

She tried not to be too disappointed. After all, he'd still suggested the beach, and they had the whole night ahead of them.

The whole night, and six more nights after that.

And then? a little voice probed. She ignored it. There was no sense getting ahead of herself. They had the week: that had to be enough.

* * *

In his room, Salvador moved slowly. He stripped out of his work clothes and dressed in some shorts and a shirt. As he approached the door, his eyes gravitated to the small, framed photo he kept on the shelf. The only family photo they'd taken: Anna-Maria, Sofia and him.

His gut churned and the hollow feeling, that was as much a part of him as his brain and blood, felt enormous and cavernous. He stopped dead in the room, staring at the photo with a visceral pain tearing through him. He was the sole survivor. When they'd taken that photo, they'd been full of hope. Sofia had been weak—the doctors had been very honest—but Salvador hadn't yet known that there were things in life his money could not buy or could not fix. That there were no guarantees.

Anna-Maria looked like herself before she'd started treatment, lost her hair and so much weight. It was a snapshot of a time before his life had gone to pieces. He moved to the picture and pressed a finger to it, guilt, pain and remorse swirling through him, so he couldn't believe that he was about to enjoy an evening of unbidden pleasures with someone as vital as Harper Lawson.

It was a betrayal in every way. Guilt cut him, but he wrapped it up into a little box and kept it buried deep inside. There would be time to feel those emotions later, time to regret and repent. For the next week, he intended to enjoy Harper, somehow understanding that being with her was essential to give him back his own sense of life, his own vitality. He needed her, he realised. Even when he didn't want to, he needed her desperately, and he wasn't strong enough to fight it—not yet, anyway.

CHAPTER TWELVE

'I could stay like this for ever!' she called over the gentle hush of the water lapping against the side of her head, the feel of it around her body like silk. It took her a moment to hear what she'd said, and the implication of those words, and she flushed to the roots of her hair. She hoped he hadn't heard and, if he had, that he didn't read anything into it.

Kicking to her feet, she stood on the sandy floor of the ocean, looking round to where Salvador had last been. He was closer now, right beside her, his expression difficult to read.

'How about the rest of the week?' he asked with a small smile that seemed relaxed enough, so he obviously hadn't interpreted her benign statement as a plea to stay longer.

Which it hadn't been. Never mind that time was passing way too fast, that they'd been back from Prague for four days now and, every minute, Harper was conscious of how close they were coming to the end of her time on the island.

'Hmm.' She pretended to consider that. 'Okay, deal.'

'Do you have any time off when you return to Chicago?'

Reality thudded against her, the prospects of the flight and return to her normal job things she didn't particularly want to contemplate. She swished her fingertips through the beautiful crystal water. 'I fly in on a Saturday night, so I'll have a day. Why?'

'It's been a busy fortnight. Perhaps you should take some leave.'

She threw him a look. 'I don't want special favours, remember?'

He lifted his hands in a gesture of surrender. 'I meant the work you've been doing here. Long days…'

'I'm used to long days.'

'Not this long.'

'No,' she agreed, moving to him so she could latch her hands behind his waist. She liked touching him. No, she loved it. Being this close to him was a form of nirvana. 'But I'll be fine. I like to be busy.' She suspected she'd *need* to be busy when she got back, if she had any hope of pushing Salvador from her mind.

'Tell me about your job.' It was a command and, like all of Salvador's commands, it sent a shiver down her spine, a wave of desire that was always inspired by his confidence and strength.

'You've seen my CV, right?' she teased.

'I know your position and title, but I mean, what do you do on a day-to-day basis?'

'Standard executive assistant duties,' she said, feeling less enthusiastic about talking than about feeling the sensuality of the moment with the water, the late-afternoon sun and his body—naked except for a pair of board shorts that she could easily dispose of…

But he was insistent. 'Such as?'

'Complex diary management, travel plans; I sit in on meetings, triage emails—a lot of the stuff I've been doing this week with you, but less of it.'

'Do you read and evaluate reports?'

'No.' Her lips twisted. 'At least, not as part of my job.'

His eyes narrowed almost imperceptibly. 'You do it because you enjoy it?'

'The reports are there. I see them. And I think it's good for me to be informed about what we're doing, so I can spot any errors.'

'I'll bet,' he said, but his jaw was clenched, his expression showing frustration. She blinked up at him, lifting a hand and brushing some wet hair back from his face.

'What is it, Salvador?'

She wondered if she'd ever stop feeling that thrill when she said his name. It felt somehow elicit.

'You're wasting yourself in a job like that.'

Her heart sped up. 'I told you, I like what I do. I'm good at it.'

'Obviously. But you could be good at anything you pursued.'

'We've discussed this. You know why I'm doing this.'

'For the money.'

'That's why most people work. Probably hard for someone like you to understand.'

'Someone like me?'

'I just mean it's been a long time since you've had to think about paying rent or the fact that hospitals cost a fortune.'

'Having money doesn't make me a moron.'

She smiled at that. 'No.'

'What if I were to give you money?' He asked the question completely deadpan, eyes hooked to hers, so she had no idea if he could read every expression that flooded her mind. He was so astute, and she feared she was like an open book to him.

'You *are* giving me money,' she said slightly unevenly, as she tried to regulate her breathing. 'The bonus I get for taking this role is huge.'

His face bore an expression of impatience. 'You've earned that.'

'Exactly.'

'I'm talking about a gift.'

'You're talking about money you wouldn't have thought to offer were it not for the fact we've been sleeping together.'

'You don't know that.'

'Oh, come on, Salvador! Of course I do.' Exasperation coloured the tone of her voice. 'You wouldn't even know about my mum if it weren't for the fact we became intimate. It's bad enough that we've…been…that this has happened… But if you were to give me money as well?' The colour drained from her face. 'I couldn't live with myself.'

'It would be a gift. No strings attached.'

She fought her wave of anger. It would be so easy

for him to do as he was suggesting and transfer a large sum of money to her. He wouldn't even notice the difference in his bank balance. The offer he was making wasn't a big deal—to him. But to Harper it was insulting and hurtful, and she couldn't even understand why she was having such a strong reaction to it, only that she knew she didn't want his money.

'The time we've spent together has been a gift,' she said slowly, earnestly. 'I don't need—or want—anything else from you.'

She knew the matter wasn't over but at least he appeared to let it go for now. 'Except the dress?' he murmured in a voice that was completely different now, light and seductive as he drew her closer to him. 'We've already discussed the fact it's not my size.'

'Okay, I'll keep the dress,' she said, as if under duress. 'If you insist.'

The only problem with the dress was that he couldn't imagine her wearing it to anything other than a date, and suddenly the idea of Harper dating some other man made Salvador's skin crawl. It was an inevitability and, hell, it was none of his business, but he couldn't get the idea of her with some creep out of his head.

It was all he could think of the next day when he should have been reading contracts his lawyers had sent over for the purchase of the hotels. There was a lot to consider, a lot of liability to wade through, and he should have been focussed one hundred per cent on the words in front of him. Instead, he saw Harper in his mind, and then, when he lifted his head for a moment, right in front of him.

If she was having the same issues, she was doing a much better job of concealing them. Her focus looked genuine. She stared at the screen, moving her fingers over the keys, frowning then typing some more, reaching for the phone, talking to someone with a smile on her face that made his gut twist and roll.

He cursed mentally and returned his gaze to the papers, reading the terms several times without taking them in.

This was impossible.

He moved to the curtains and closed them, boxing himself into his office, but unfortunately not pushing Harper even part way from his mind. Or the fact they had two more nights together.

'This is delicious,' Harper murmured, barely able to taste the lobster the chef had prepared. It was their second-last night together and the knowledge of that kept rushing through her like a drum, over and over. *Two more nights. Two more nights.* In Prague, when she'd thought they might just have one night together, it had seemed like enough. A one-night stand, as heaps of people experimented with.

But, the more time she spent with Salvador, the greedier she was for him, the hungrier for more time, laughs, conversation, sex and everything. She loved being with him, here on this island or travelling. She just loved…this.

Her eyes stung a little and she had the mortifying

realisation that she was close to tears…so close. She stabbed a piece of lobster in the creamy sauce and lifted it to her lips, forcing a smile as she finished chewing.

'Tell me about this, Salvador,' she said, command in her voice for a change.

He put down his fork, relaxing in the chair, apparently not surfing any of the emotional currents she was; his expression was perfectly normal. 'The lobster? I know only that it was once in the ocean.'

She pouted. 'I mean, this…' She gestured to the house, then the island and the silhouette of the rainforest that led to the beach. 'How does a man your age come to be so successful?'

'That's a matter of public record. I invested wisely.'

She reached for her wine glass, taking a sip, glad they were talking, because it distracted her mind from the inevitability of her departure, and more than anything she needed to be distracted.

'But with what? I know you're "self-made", because that's part of the company's bio,' she said without thinking, then realised it showed she'd researched him a little. 'It was part of my job application,' she supplied quickly. 'I had to demonstrate knowledge of da Rocha Industries.'

'And here I thought you'd had a burning passion for me all this time,' he responded with a smile. There was silence except for the pleasant song of night birds swooping through the trees, making merry, and then Salvador's deep voice. 'I owe it all to my mother, actually.'

Harper lifted a brow, curious about that. 'In what way?'

'She taught me to manage money well. She also had

excellent instincts,' he continued. 'We would discuss investments even when I was just a boy.'

'She came from money?'

He shook his head, eyes glittered with so much pride it blew Harper away when his gaze met hers. 'No. Quite the opposite. My mother was dirt-poor. She worked as a cleaner at a hotel in Rio. The man she conceived me with was in town for a few weeks—on holiday,' Salvador said with a voice mute of emotion. 'She fell in love. He saw an opportunity to have some fun while his wife was at home in Sydney, raising their children.'

Harper's lips parted. It was so like her own experience, she felt an immediate rush of sympathy for his mother. 'I'm very sorry for her. That's an awful feeling.'

'Like you, she had no idea he was married. He didn't choose to enlighten her, and was gone before she realised she was pregnant.'

'Awful.' Harper shook her head sadly.

'She was able to get his number through the hotel records.'

'And?'

Salvador ran a finger down the side of his beer glass, eyes fixed on the drink rather than Harper. 'When she told him about me, he denied that I could possibly be his. He accused her of trying to ruin his life, his marriage, and in order to ensure her silence he offered her a reasonably obscene amount of money in exchange for the signing of a non-disclosure.'

Harper gaped. 'You're kidding! And she loved him?'

'Up until that moment, she thought she did. She hadn't seen what he was truly like. He was a spoiled, entitled son of a very successful Sydney real-estate mogul. He grew up with money at his fingertips and thought he could use it to pay people off.' Salvador shook his head angrily.

'What did your mother do?'

'Took his money.' Salvador's expression showed pride. 'She grew up tough. She knew he'd never change his mind—he'd never be a father to me, and besides she didn't want him in my life after that. She took the money, signed the damned agreement and she worked her fingers to the bone to make a success of her life. She continued to work as a housekeeper until I was born, by which point she'd bought a couple of apartments that earned her a rental income so she could stay home with me. It snowballed from there.'

'She sounds like an amazing woman.'

'She was.'

'She's gone?'

He sipped his drink. 'She died when I was in my early twenties.'

She reached out and put her hand over his, feeling the reliable hum of connection that came whenever they touched. 'Did you ever reach out to your father?'

'He's not my father.'

She dipped her head in silent concession to that.

'I had no interest in knowing him. Any man who can treat a woman like that...' He shook his head. 'What could I possibly want from him?'

Harper agreed completely, but still she marvelled at Salvador's restraint. 'You must have wanted to...'

'He was never a part of my life. Besides a little DNA,

I am nothing to do with him. It is because of his choices, though, that I married.'

Harper's heart stitched painfully. 'Oh?' It was the best she could manage. The existence of his late wife was a matter of fact, and Harper knew it wasn't right to feel jealous of Anna-Maria—but how could she not?

'When Anna-Maria fell pregnant, I had only one choice: to offer to marry her. Unlike the man my mother loved, I wanted to be an active father. To know and love my child every day of their life. I also wanted to support my baby's mother.'

She stared at him as if from a thousand miles away. 'I'm sorry. Did you just say…?'

'Anna-Maria was pregnant.' He spoke quietly, as if repeating words learned by rote. 'We only slept together that once. The pregnancy was a complete surprise.'

Harper could hardly breathe. She'd been so curious about his wife, his marriage, his life before she'd known him, but she hadn't expected any of this. They'd only slept together once…even after they'd married? Her heart rabbited into her chest and she leaned forward unconsciously.

'I offered to marry her immediately. I wanted to raise my child. It was important to me—more important than to most, I suspect—because of the abandonment of the man my mother had dated. But it was more than that. Anna-Maria and I had grown up together. We *knew* each other, loved each other as old, close friends. Marriage made sense.'

Harper nodded sympathetically, her throat too thick to allow the formation of words. He'd loved her…

as a friend. She was trying to put the pieces together, to understand.

'She agreed, obviously?'

'Not at first. She hated the idea of feeling that she'd "trapped" me. She knew about my dad, knew why I reacted as I did.'

'I can understand that.' Harper sipped her wine. 'So what happened?'

'I convinced her,' he said. 'Quite quickly. We married a few months later—before Sofia was born.'

She could imagine how persuasive Salvador would be once he set his mind to something. 'What happened to Sofia, Salvador?' She was almost afraid to ask.

He clenched his jaw, leaning back in his chair and looking in the direction of the ocean. The moon was behind a cloud tonight.

'When Anna-Maria went for her three-month scan, they found a mass—she had cancer. The doctors wanted her to have an abortion, to begin treatment immediately—it would have been the only hope for her survival.'

Harper gasped. It was all too sad. 'I can't even imagine how hard that must have been.'

'She refused.' Salvador's voice was like a vice. Harper wanted to tell him they could stop talking about this, but at the same time she felt he needed to say these words, and she owed it to him to listen. 'There was no way she was going to lose our baby.'

'Of course,' Harper murmured.

'No.' Salvador's eyes glittered. 'Not *of course*. I told her we could try again, once she was all better. I told her we could have ten more babies, that she had to survive this, but Anna-Maria refused. She said that when she was gone it would give her comfort to know I had our daughter. And God, Harper, how I admired her strength. She sacrificed *everything* for Sofia. Everything.'

Harper's chest hurt. She felt so much affection for Anna-Maria then, for her goodness and kindness, her loving heart.

'When she was at seven months' gestation, the doctors said it was time to induce labour. The baby was big enough—they'd put her on oxygen and begin treatment immediately. By then, Anna-Maria's cancer was spreading rapidly. She'd felt her baby move, and she wanted to be here for our little girl, as much as I wanted her to be.'

Harper sobbed. She couldn't help it. Salvador didn't seem to notice. He was in the past, reliving memories that must have been truly traumatic.

'When Sofia was born, she was utterly perfect but so tiny. Like a little quail, all dainty and bony. She lived for a week.' He said the last words so matter-of-factly, and that was more devastating than if he'd broken down into floods of tears. 'Anna-Maria got to hold our baby, to love her, but that was all. Just three months later, Anna-Maria died.'

He turned to face Harper then, piercing her with the desperation in his eyes.

'They're buried together, here on the island. This was where Anna-Maria was happiest.'

Harper's chest hurt. She couldn't bear it. Standing, she moved over to Salvador and sat in his lap, clutching his face with her hands as tears streamed down her cheeks. She ached for him, for all he'd gone through and for the pain he'd felt. She didn't know how a person could ever recover from that.

And then, it hit her. He hadn't recovered. He was broken, completely destroyed by the loss of his wife and daughter, by the blows fate had dealt him. That was why he walled himself away on this island, why he wouldn't get involved with anyone else. It wasn't just love for his late wife, it was the fear of losing someone he cared about all over again. Even his father's rejection must have shaped his view on life, on people and the unreliable nature of affection.

She knew then why this mattered so much to her. Why she cared so much.

She loved him.

She loved Salvador da Rocha, and the fact he'd turned his heart to stone through sheer willpower alone would have a lasting impact on Harper's life.

'I wish I could fix this for you,' she said quietly, pressing her forehead to his, needing him to hear that. She wished with all her heart that she knew how to make him whole again… She dropped a hand to his chest, pressing it to his heart, wishing that with touch alone she could do just that.

His response was to tilt his face and capture her lips with his, to kiss her as though he was in free fall and she his only touchstone, and she let him, because they both needed this. They needed each other and the connection that came from making love.

Salvador shifted, as though waking from a dream, but he hadn't been asleep. Rather, he'd been possessed. He'd had a need to take Harper here on the terrace, where any member of staff could have walked out and witnessed them. The urgency had driven his hands, his body, to push aside her underpants beneath her dress, unzip his fly and push into her, taking her, because it was the only way to blot the grief from his mind, to feel human again, rather than a spectre of the losses that had shaped him for years now.

He blinked up at Harper, seeing the way her face was illuminated by the soft lighting of the terrace, her eyes still shimmering with unspent tears, and he felt a piece of him break apart—a piece he'd never get back.

This time with Harper had been beyond words, but it had to end. He was losing himself in her, losing himself *to* her, and the risks were simply too great.

CHAPTER THIRTEEN

THE SUN ROSE in a spectacular show of colour, streaks of orange, pink and purple bursting into the sky. The trees beyond the house were the deepest green, their early-morning noises evocative of newness and renewal. Harper blinked out at the view, her heart skipping a beat because she loved this place, almost as much as she loved the man beside her.

Only Salvador wasn't beside her, she realised, reaching out and feeling the empty bed sheets, which were cool to the touch. He'd been gone a while.

Her heart made another strange twist, a jerk in her chest, but she told herself not to panic.

She was feeling uneasy because it was her last full day here. One more night and she'd fly back to the mainland, and then onto Chicago, and all this would be a distant memory. A whole host of them, in fact, memories she would hold close to her heart for ever.

But what if you didn't go?

She paused midway through pushing out of bed and stared at the wall opposite which was creamy white with a huge painting of a floral arrangement in the style of the Dutch masters.

What was the alternative to going? Staying with Salvador? Her heart was pummelling her now, racing hard and fast. She *couldn't* just stay here with him. She had no idea how he'd feel about that. He'd never once expressed any interest in having her stay longer. He hadn't suggested it, hadn't asked—they'd both acknowledged her impending leaving date time and time again.

And did Harper really want to stay? What would happen then? Wouldn't it just be kicking the can down the road to remain on the island for another few nights, a week, two weeks, however long they agreed they needed before they'd be ready for her to leave? The problem with that was that Harper didn't think she'd ever be ready to leave him. She pressed the back of her hand to her mouth, smothering a sharp cry drawn from the very pit of her stomach.

If she asked to stay, it would be because she wanted to stay for ever. And if he said no she would never recover.

But what if he says yes?

She groaned, tears of frustration and uncertainty blinking on her lashes. She loved him, and the thought of rejection was terrifying, but wouldn't she always regret not having that conversation? If she were to return to Chicago and go on with her life—as half a person, really, because she'd left so much of herself here with Salvador—she'd always wonder what might have been, if only she'd been brave enough to speak up about how she felt.

And what if he does say yes?

And so she'd stay, and her heart would belong to him, more fully than her mother's heart had ever belonged to anyone, more than Harper had ever given herself to Peter. Wasn't there a terrifying risk in that? A risk of pain and hurt of a level capable of ripping her to shreds... And yet, there was no alternative.

Harper was a risk-taker by nature, an adrenaline junkie who knew that the sheer moments of fear one experienced when jumping out of a plane or off the side of a bridge were nothing to the feeling of having done it—and survived.

She would survive this. Whatever happened, she'd be okay, but she had to take the leap, to know she'd at least reached for what she wanted with both hands, even if it didn't work out.

'There you are,' she murmured half an hour later, when she walked onto the terrace to find Salvador sitting with a cup of black coffee and a tablet in front of him with the newspaper on it.

He turned slowly, as if reading something he couldn't quite tear his eyes away from, but there was something in the gesture that didn't quite ring true for Harper. He was avoiding her. Or steeling himself to see her?

The sun was higher now, the sky blue with just a few streaks of morning colour remaining. She moved to the seat opposite but didn't sit down, instead pressing her hands to the back of it and eyeing him a little warily, her stomach in knots as she geared herself up for the most important conversation of her life.

'You left early.'

He made a noise of agreement, eyes piercing hers. If she was wary, he was even more so, but it was an insight into his emotions that only lasted a moment. He controlled his features far more easily than Harper, shielding his feelings from her, his face a mask of impassive politeness.

Her heart dropped to her toes. It was a feeling she was familiar with—the fear before the jump. The doubt, the very natural questioning of one's wisdom.

'I couldn't sleep and didn't want to wake you.'

'I wouldn't have minded being woken,' she murmured, a half-smile flickering across her lips. She suspected this wasn't going to go well when we he frowned in response.

He was sitting where he had been last night, when he'd told her about his wife, his daughter and his father, so much loss, rejection and pain. But, whereas last night he'd opened up to her and she'd seen so deep inside his soul, now he was like a boulder, immovable and strong—and impenetrable too, she feared.

'Would you like some coffee?' He gestured to the pot. There was no second cup but either of them could have retrieved one easily. While Harper would have loved something to do with her hands, she couldn't have eaten or drunk anything. Her nerves were rioting, her insides completely tangled.

'I'm fine,' she demurred, wondering when she'd ever felt less fine. It was unusual to be out here. Generally, they both went into the office first thing. But this morning, their last full day together on the island, even the air seemed changed.

She closed her eyes, just as she did when psyching herself into a jump. 'Can we talk?'

She could barely look at him.

'Aren't we talking?'

This was going to go down like a lead balloon. But when she remembered the last two weeks—the way he'd pushed her away even as he'd drawn her closer, when he'd tried so hard to fight what was happening between them—she saw this as yet another last-ditch attempt by him to exert some kind of control over what was happening between them.

'About us.' She forced herself to meet and hold his gaze even when she felt as though she could pass out from the anxiety of having this conversation. No, not of having the conversation, but of what could go wrong.

'Us?'

Her heart skidded to a stop. It was only by reminding herself that he had form for this—for running away from their relationship when things got real—that she was able to push on and be brave.

'Yes, us. You and me, and what's been happening between us.'

He stared at her without reacting. She gripped the chair back more tightly, so tightly that her fingers burned and her knuckles showed white.

'This was always meant to be temporary,' she said, mentally approaching the edge of the plane, looking out at the vastness of open air, then down to the ground, her stomach looping as she imagined the feeling of pushing both feet from the security of the flight deck.

'You leave tomorrow,' he pointed out, voice unmoving.

'Yes. I think we both took some kind of assurance from the end date we've been moving towards. It saved us from having to have any conversations about what we wanted, about when and how and why this would end.'

A slight frown shifted his lips.

'Haven't we discussed that?'

She ignored the question. He was pushing hard. She should have expected it. Even knowing *why* he was like this didn't soften the feelings of hurt. She inhaled and exhaled, her breath a little shaky.

'I think that what we have is really good, Salvador.' She cleared her throat, eyes stinging, but she refused to give in to tears. 'I don't want it to end yet.'

She saw his response. Something shifted in the depths of his eyes, and his throat moved as he swallowed, but he didn't speak. Not at first. He was pulling his thoughts together, sifting through what he felt and wanted, and what he wanted to say.

'You're leaving in the morning,' he pointed out again with the appearance of calm.

'But what if I didn't?' she asked with more urgency, because he was making this so damned hard. If he was going to reject her, she wanted to just rip the plaster off now. She came round to him, putting a hand on his shoulder to draw his attention up to her face. He hesitated and then looked into her eyes. She shivered, because he was holding onto his willpower with the strength of a thousand men.

'What if you didn't what, Harper?'

'Leave. Tomorrow.' She moistened her lower lip then continued, even as she was pretty sure what was going to happen. 'What if I stayed here with you?'

He stood abruptly, placing his coffee on the table, the sudden movement an indication that he *was* feeling something in response to this conversation.

'For how long?' he asked, the words reverberating with barely contained anger.

She closed her eyes against the wave of pain. 'I don't know.' It was an honest response. 'For as long as it felt right.' Harper knew for her that would be for the rest of her life, but she was too scared to admit as much now.

'But that's the problem,' he said slowly, eyes like stone when they met hers, none of the golden light shining for her. 'This doesn't feel right to me. It's everything I swore I didn't want.'

'Which is what?' she asked, trying to ignore her own pain and sadness to concentrate on the logic of his statement. 'Utterly alone?'

He compressed his lips. 'You knew this about me.'

'Yes,' she agreed unevenly. 'But then there was Prague.' She frowned, shaking her head. 'That's not right. It was before Prague. It was the first moment we met. You felt it too, I know you did, and it only got more and more obvious the more time we spent together.'

'Felt what?'

She reached across and pressed her hand to his heart.

'This connection.' She blinked up at him, so much hope in her face.

'Desire?' he countered. 'Is it any wonder? I've been celibate for two years. Since that one damned night with Anna-Maria. And then you arrived, so willing, and naturally I responded. Don't mistake sex for anything more.'

She gasped. He'd said something like this before, but now it cut her deep to her soul. She tried to hold onto her certainty that he was pushing her away because he couldn't cope with the things he felt, the emotions coursing through his veins. But at some point she had to hear his words and realise that, whatever reason he had for issuing them, he was a grown man capable of conveying what he wanted to convey. And, right now, that was a huge, 'no thanks' to Harper's suggestion.

She pulled her hand away, spinning so she could regain her breath and mind and control the tears that were making her throat sting.

'Just to be clear,' she said unevenly—because she knew she'd need to recall this later when she was wondering if there was more she could have said or done, if maybe she'd misunderstood him. 'You're saying that what we shared was nothing special. That, if any other woman you were halfway attracted to had been here on Ilha do Sonhos with you, you'd have slept with them, because it's been so long since you've had sex. That's what I was to you?'

She couldn't look at him. She couldn't turn, so didn't see the way his features tightened, the way he recoiled a little at her words.

'It was sex,' he said finally. 'Great sex. But I was clear with you all along, and no amount of sex is going to change who I am.'

Sex. Just sex. *Great sex,* she thought with an angry tilt of her lips, tears sparkling on her lashes.

'Okay,' she said after a pause. 'Good to know.'

Harper could have changed her flight—she had the ability to make all the arrangements herself—but leaving work, even one day early, was something her pride wouldn't allow her to do. So she sat at her desk and went through the long list of things she'd wanted to check before Amanda's return the following day, ensuring she left clear notes of what she'd done and why, explaining anything that was still to be resolved.

It was painstaking work, because her mind was in shards, and because Salvador sat in the office next door, near but so far. Because he could see her and she refused to allow him to know how much she was hurting, so she worked without a break, without looking up from her computer screen. But as the day drew on and she recognised the end was in sight, that she'd almost got through the long list of jobs on her list, she knew she couldn't stay on this island a moment longer than was professionally necessary.

She was meant to fly out the following morning, but there was no point in remaining for one extra night. With a huge lump in her throat, she opened the travel-booking browser and put in a request for a change of flight—from Rio that evening with the same helicopter pilot booked to return her who'd flown her over to the island. Once she had the confirmation email, she knew it was the right decision.

He didn't want her to stay.

He didn't see any value in what they'd shared beyond great sex. One more night wasn't going to change anything.

She ploughed through her work, completing everything, tidying her desk, aware that Salvador could be watching her at all times, so being very careful to keep her expression neutral before she moved to the area that joined their offices.

She thought about leaving without saying goodbye, without explanation. Technically, she'd completed her contract, what she'd been hired to do. But, while he'd been comfortable reducing their relationship to something simple and one-dimensional, Harper knew that what they'd shared deserved more from her.

Changing direction, she moved to his door and knocked once. He took a few seconds to stop what he was doing and look up. She ground her teeth and didn't enter his office—too much his space, with his masculine fragrance. She realised that she'd never been in his bedroom, and wondered why she hadn't questioned that. It was yet another example of Salvador keeping a part of himself separate from her, walled off, showing her she didn't mean enough to get all of him.

Whereas she would have given him her soul.

'I just wanted to let you know that I'm leaving in an hour.'

Whatever response he would have made, he concealed too quickly for her to comprehend. Silence prickled her skin, stretching for several moments before he nodded once. 'That's fine.'

She glared at him. 'I wasn't asking for your permission.'

More silence, throbbing now—angry, hurt. She hated that she felt like this. She hated that she'd let another man do this to her. Digging her nails into her palm, she knew she had to hold on to her temper, her rage and her hurt, until she was off the island. Her pride wouldn't allow her to show how badly he'd affected her.

'What do you want me to say, Harper?' he said, his mouth a grim line. 'That I'm sorry? I am. I didn't mean for you to get hurt. I truly thought you understood me, and what I could offer. We both knew you would leave and that would be the end of it.'

She looked away from him, turning her face to profile. He was like a different person. She didn't recognise this Salvador, but maybe that was her mistake. He was renowned for his toughness and strength. She'd even heard him described as ruthless before, but Harper had discounted that once she'd come to know him. But maybe she hadn't really known him at all. Maybe she'd been wrong about him all along, just as with Peter. She was a naïve, trusting fool.

The bottom seemed to be falling out of her world. She had to get the hell out of there.

'I don't think I understood you before, but I do now,' she said with a quiet strength that would form the backbone of Salvador's nightmares for many nights to follow. She took a moment to settle her rioting emotions, so she could speak without a wobbling voice. 'I've left detailed instructions for Amanda. There shouldn't be any issues, but naturally she can call me with whatever she needs.' She hesitated for a beat. 'Goodbye.'

'Goodbye' had such finality.

Goodbye was an ending. A permanent sunset. Not a reprieve, not a temporary farewell.

Just as he wanted, he reminded himself, watching the clock on his computer counting down the hour, knowing he wouldn't be able to breathe properly until he'd heard the helicopter leave and knew she was gone.

Every minute until then was filled with indecision, an uncharacteristic doubt permeating every cell in his body.

How could he let her go?

How could he let her stay?

He felt as if he'd been felled at the knees. After forty-five minutes, he gave up staring at the time and closed his laptop, instead moving to the expansive windows of his office, staring out at the view of the hills, the forest, the dazzling ocean in the distance and far beyond that Rio… Salvador's eyes hunted reprieve and peace, when there was none available to him.

What he needed was to obliterate his senses. Not to think, not to feel, not to imagine Harper packing her bag, tidying her room, boarding a helicopter and preparing to leave.

With a gruff sound, he pushed the chair against his desk and stalked out of his office. There was only one place he could be right now, and it sure as hell wasn't here.

* * *

She'd half-expected, hoped, he'd come after her. There
was no way he'd let her walk away like this. Not after
what they'd shared. Not after what they'd meant to each
other.

And they *did* mean something to each other; she
knew they did. She hadn't imagined their connection.
This was real and it was true, but one person couldn't
love another enough to make a relationship work. Taking one last look back at the house, high up on the
hill away from civilisation and the coastline, Harper
boarded the helicopter. It was identical to the one that
had brought her here two weeks ago, when she'd been
filled with a rush of adrenaline at the challenge that lay
ahead. She couldn't have known that being here would
fundamentally change who she was inside.

The sun was setting as Harper lifted off the island,
the colours stunning, striking, as the morning had been.
So she thought about that—the way these displays book-
ended life here on the island—and tears that she'd been
fighting all day finally began to fall down her cheeks.
Were they book-ends? Or signs of perennial hope? The
sun would set and night would follow, dark and long,
but always there'd be morning, a glow streaking across
the sky offering a renewal. Was it always the case that
day followed night? Hope followed darkness? Or could
some nights be so long and so permeating that there
was no escape from them, even when morning came?

Harper was about to find out.

CHAPTER FOURTEEN

THE WAVES CRASHED down on Salvador, hard and angrily, just as he'd wanted, here on the southern tip of the island where the ocean buffeted it hard. He'd wanted to drown out everything, but especially the sound of the helicopter leaving. But at the same time his ears were subconsciously straining to hear it, so he turned and saw it as it left the pad, lifting up with blades flapping, taking its sole passenger, Harper, away from Ilha do Sonhos, away from Salvador, away for ever.

It was what he'd wanted. What he'd known was necessary.

A wave pummelled him and Salvador was glad. After all he'd been through, all he'd lost, it was in that moment he truly felt he'd hit rock bottom.

Salvador took an extra interest in Harper's department after that. It was an obsession that he fully recognised was a little sick. After all, she'd offered to stay here with him, where he could have had his fill of her, held her, laughed with her, watched her working and walked with her. But he'd sent her away, unequivocally shutting down any prospect of a relationship, of a future, of anything beyond what they'd shared.

It was sex.

He shuddered, remembering the way Harper had recoiled and the light in her eyes had dimmed, the pain of his brutal appraisal rocking her to her core.

He'd sent her away when she would have stayed, so it made no sense that now he pored over reports from her department, looking for signs of her handiwork and seeing very little. Frustration twisted through him. Why was she being so under-utilised within the company? She'd gone toe to toe with Salvador, working at his pace, totally his equal in every way. There was so much more she could be doing than juggling someone's diary.

Okay, he knew her job was more complicated than that, but it was obvious that she'd settled for a job she could do standing on her head because it paid well.

Her financial needs had him sitting up straighter. When she'd spoken of her mother, he'd felt the fierceness of her love. But, apart from a mother who lay in a nursing home, who did Harper have?

Salvador had been so focussed on his own solitary life that he hadn't stopped to think about Harper. About how she'd also lost the people she loved.

And now Salvador had added to that burden. He was someone else who'd hurt her and left her. Someone else who'd done the wrong thing by her, taking what he wanted while it had suited him then pushing her away because he didn't want to fight for something that might end up destroying him.

He swore, standing, dragging frantic hands through his hair, needing to escape Harper properly but knowing he couldn't. In the three weeks since she'd left, he'd travelled widely and she'd followed him. She was a fixture in his mind all the time.

How could he ever escape her? And did he really want to?

Harper had it down pat now. At first, she'd struggled big time. But after three weeks she knew how to go through the motions adequately enough to fool everyone into thinking she was okay. The trick was to perfectly emulate how she'd been before.

She caught the same train, she wore the same clothes, packed the same lunch, made the same meaningless conversations, walked the same way, called or went to see her mum at the same time as usual. She held the act together just until she walked in her front door each night and could finally give into her state of grief.

It wasn't that her heart was broken. That was too simple. Her heart was in a permanent state of breakage, each breath hurting it more and more, each memory like a fresh blade to her flesh, so she was in literal pain all day, all night—all the time. She couldn't exist without thinking of Salvador, without missing him, and that had become a part of her, stitched into her being. But after three weeks she'd learned to fake it adequately enough so that she could walk through her day without anyone else knowing that she'd gone to Ilha do Sonhos and come back into a living nightmare.

* * *

It was the middle of the night when he woke, disturbed by fragments of dreams that shook him up and threw him into a strange, warped past so he couldn't quite piece together what was real and what was a memory.

His mother was there, in a white linen dress, her long, dark hair coiled in a bun at her nape, a caipirinha in her hand and a smile on her face as the sun dipped towards the blanket of the ocean, dragging night in its wake.

'Ilha do Sonhos—Isle of Dreams. Don't you think it's appropriate, *mei filho*?'

Salvador was a twenty-year-old again, arrogant and full of determination to make his mark, to prove to his father, who he never intended to meet, what a mistake he'd made in not wanting Salvador.

'It's a beautiful place.'

'But the dreams.' Her smile was mystical. 'Here, on this island, I feel like anything is possible. Don't you see it? Don't you feel it?'

'I feel warm.' He shrugged.

'No, Salvador. You're not doing it properly. Close your eyes.'

He refused at first, but his mother insisted.

'See?' she asked, her voice lyrical and light.

'No.'

'There's magic here. It's in the air as you breathe, it's in the forest and the waves. And it's in the setting of the sun and the stirring of the new day. This island is a gift. Never forget that.'

'It's an island.' He laughed.

'But here, it's a reminder that all things are possible. Look around us now. Look at this. How can you see this beauty and doubt the truth of that?'

Back in his bedroom now, sheets tangled as evidence of a disrupted night's sleep, his heart was racing. That had just been one fragment of his dream, though. Anna-Maria had been there too, as she'd been towards the end, on the last visit they'd made to Sofia's grave. She'd been so beautiful and ethereal, as though she'd been halfway to assuming an angel's form.

'You have to live for us, Salvador.' She took his hand in hers, fingers so fine he wanted to cry. 'There is no meaning to her death, or mine, unless you give it to us. I don't mean by naming a library after me, or building a statue here in this garden,' she teased, then paused to cough, because she was faint of breath all the time.

Salvador waited patiently, not asking if she was okay, because she hated that. Instead, he pressed a hand reassuringly to her back, wincing as he felt her spine through the fabric of her clothes, knowing she had a very limited number of breaths left to draw—this woman who'd once been a girl he'd run with until their lungs had burned and their cheeks had been flame-red, who'd once been as vital and real as the nights were dark.

'Every day, you have to do something for me. Live your life in a way I would be proud of. Make decisions that prove you're alive, because I won't be. And she never really got to be.' A tear slid down Anna-Maria's cheek and Salvador wanted the world to open up and swallow him into the pits of its lava-filled belly. 'You owe it to us.'

He wiped his forehead now, which was covered in perspiration, then pushed back the sheets, planting both feet over the edge of the bed and leaning forward, elbows braced on his knees and his head cradled in his palms.

Because Harper had been there too.

He dreamed of her as she'd been on that last morning. Not of the words she'd said, but the smile she'd offered when she'd first arrived. It was a smile that had haunted him, over and over, and now he understood, finally, why that was.

Her smile had been like a sunrise. A beautiful, hope-filled, promise-laden, glorious gift, reassuring and bright after the longest night of his life, a grief-soaked slumber from which he thought he'd never stir. Ilha do Sonhos—Isle of Dreams. Magic was everywhere and anything was possible.

He'd already failed the two most important women in his life—his mother and Anna-Maria—by failing to abide by his promises to them.

And now, he'd done exactly the same thing to Harper. Because he had made her a promise, he realised, lifting his face and looking towards the window, surprise changing his features. He'd never told her he loved her, but surely he'd shown her with every conversation, with the way he'd tried to push her away but had instead ended up pulling her closer again and again?

He'd made her a thousand little promises every moment that she'd been here and then he'd rejected her because he'd been terrified of what allowing her to stay would mean. How could he have let her stay when that would have meant opening the door to a world that would contain so many risks…? But what was the alternative?

He cursed as he stood, striding across his room with renewed purpose and dressing swiftly.

It wasn't just about a promise to Harper, though. It was about how he felt and what he wanted. It was about pushing through the fear of losing her because every day he had with her would be a gift and he was willing to go through any eventual pain for just one more day, one more kiss. For a little bit of hope and that sunrise smile of hers…if she'd offer it to him again.

'Harper, would you get the boardroom ready?'

Midway through replying to an email, she paused what she was doing to look at her boss, Jack Wotton, as he propped an arm against the door to her office.

'Sure thing. Meeting?'

'Unexpected, but yes.' He looked a little nervous, which was definitely out of character.

'What's the problem?' Harper asked, just wanting to be home. She was tired. Tired of pretending to be fine, tired of pretending she was okay when she absolutely wasn't. It was Friday and she had two days of blissful alone time ahead when she could switch off and stop pretending. When she could wallow in her sadness and loneliness and not have to pretend for anyone else.

'No problem. I hope.' Jack's brow was furrowed.

'Jack?'

'It's Salvador da Rocha. He's coming here. I'm sure everything's just at it should be. I just wish I knew what it was about.'

Harper jerked so hard she whacked her knee into the side of her desk and the breath in her lungs burned as she exhaled.

'When?' The word shot from her lips with panicked urgency.

'Half an hour.'

She looked at her watch. It was almost five. 'Jack, I have an appointment,' she lied, grabbing her bag and placing it on her desk. 'I'll set up the conference room but then I have to go straight away. Do you mind?'

'I'd prefer you stayed and took minutes—'

The very idea made Harper's insides squelch in pain. Seeing Salvador, sharing a room with him…?

She shook her head emphatically, swallowing and reaching for her phone. 'I'll ask David to do it. He owes me a favour.' Then she said reassuringly to Jack, because wild horses wouldn't make her stay in this building a moment longer, 'He's very good, don't worry. Everything will be fine.'

The final reassurance, she added for her own benefit. *Everything will be fine. Everything will be fine.* So long as she got the hell out of there.

But in the end it took longer than expected to set up the meeting room, courtesy of the previous occupants having left coffee cups and old papers lying around. Harper worked as quickly as she could, all the while conscious of the ticking of time and her desperate need to escape. Finally, with only minutes to spare, she finished and zipped into Jack's office.

'I have to go,' she said breathlessly, pulling her bag over her shoulder. 'Good luck.'

'Thanks.' He didn't look up and Harper was glad. She couldn't imagine how pale her face would have looked if he'd given her a moment's thought. She needed to escape: now.

CHAPTER FIFTEEN

SALVADOR HAD NEVER particularly liked the way he was
treated when he travelled to his offices. As the head of
a billion-dollar company that employed tens of thou-
sands of people worldwide, he understood it a little,
but being deified wasn't his idea of a good time, so he
avoided this sort of thing as much as possible.

Meetings could be done offsite or online.

But this wasn't really about a meeting, so much as
a chance to see Harper on her terms. To *see her*, he
thought with a clutch in his chest. Though how the hell
he could see her without reaching for her, without kissing her senseless, without blurting out everything he'd
realised since she'd left the island, was beyond him.

His hands formed fists at his side as the lift whooshed
towards the executive level of his Chicago high-rise.
Blessedly, he was alone. He needed the few moments
to steel himself for this, for seeing her at her desk, just
as she'd been on the island for so much of the time.

What he wasn't prepared for was the doors opening
directly into the foyer and Harper standing waiting for
a lift. She was looking at the numbers on the top of the

panel, so he had a few seconds to study her before her gaze swooped down, a few seconds to see how pale she was, how pinched were her features, how dark were her eyes. And in those few seconds he died a slow and tor- turous death, because he understood why she looked like that—he was the cause.

It was because of him.

Unless something else had happened. Something with her mother? Worry pushed aside his own feelings for a moment, and then her eyes met his and once more he understood. This *was* because of him. Nothing else could explain the jolt of emotions that flooded her face as comprehension dawned and she recognised him.

She looked like a terrified animal, haunted and hunted, and he groaned, pain stabbing his side.

'Harper...' He held up a placating hand but she could only shake her head, her lips moving without making sound, her fingers trembling as she lifted one hand to her handbag strap and yanked on it hard. It was excru- ciating to see her react like this, but this was Harper Lawson—she was made of steel—so she closed her eyes and, when she opened them again, she looked more like herself. The shock was gone, or at least concealed be- hind a look of bored impatience.

'Jack's waiting for you,' she said crisply, gesturing to the foyer.

Salvador swallowed. The meeting had essentially just been a ruse to get close to Harper again, but he stepped out of the lift, noticing the way she moved away from him and took a circuitous route to the cubicle he'd just occupied, jabbing the button for the ground-floor lobby impatiently, her face pale once more, her eyes showing shock. He stared at her and imagined the doors closing, imagined her disappearing, and realised he didn't know where she lived and he didn't have her mobile number. He had only her work email address, which was a pretty inadequate way to contact someone about a personal matter.

Just as the doors began to close, he made a split-second decision and slipped through them, eyes meeting hers, challenging her to say something, his expression carefully contained so she wouldn't know just how terrified he was of the next few moments.

'Mr da Rocha,' she said sternly, but the impression was hampered by the fact her voice trembled slightly. 'Jack is waiting for you. You should go.'

He couldn't relax until the lift doors closed. He figured he had maybe thirty seconds to say what he wanted to say before they reached the ground floor. Harper closed her eyes, blocking him out.

Thirty seconds would never be enough.

'I came here to see you.'

It wasn't the most elegant place to start but it was something.

Her jaw worked overtime as she computed that, swallowing and feeling without emoting anything.

'I should never have spoken to you the way I did on that last day. What we shared was…'

The lift slowed, stopped and the doors pinged open, admitting four more people, talking and laughing until they saw Salvador da Rocha, and then they were silent, awestruck. He glared at them mutinously—did they have any idea what they'd just interrupted? His eyes shifted to Harper but she was looking ahead resolutely, staring at the metallic underbelly of the doors as if she could will the carriage to the ground faster, if only she concentrated hard enough.

The lift reached the foyer without making any additional stops and Harper stepped out in front of him, walking quickly across the tiled entrance. He walked after her, ignoring the looks people sent him, ignoring anyone who came close to thinking they might start a conversation.

She said goodnight to the security guards then pushed through the swirling glass doors, so he followed in a vacant space behind her. Only once they were in the cold night air—so frigid compared to the island— did Salvador call her name.

Harper didn't turn. The pavement was bustling with people leaving the office, beginning their commutes home. Frustrated, and terrified of losing her now he was so close to her, he reached out, catching her wrist and pulling her to a stop. She didn't fight him. She paused, an island in the midst of the swirling sea of people. But he had to tug on her wrist again to get her to turn to him and, when she did, it felt as if every part of him was cracking apart.

Tears filmed her lashes and she just looked so inconsolably sad, so awfully hurt, that he groaned.

'I'm sorry.' He said the only thing he could think of in that moment, and it was an apology that was dredged from the very bottom of his soul. 'I had no right to talk to you the way I did. Nothing I said that day was

true, Harper. You know that. You know that in here.'
He pressed a hand to his own heart, remembering how
she'd touched him there and he'd felt as though they
were connected on a cellular level.

She blinked quickly, trying to look in control, but
she couldn't, so she gave up. 'Let me go.'

God, he knew he should. He knew he had no right
to hold her like this, to keep her here, but he couldn't
risk losing her. 'Will you come with me?' he asked ur-
gently, wiping his thumb over her inner wrist.

'No.'

He was losing her. Maybe he'd already lost her. And
didn't he deserve that? Salvador had always excelled
at everything he attempted. Being naturally good at
things was Salvador's gift in life, so was it any surprise that in trying to push Harper away he'd well and
truly succeeded?

'We need to have a conversation,' he said, looking
around and scanning the street. 'Will you at least step
this way so we're out of the flow of people?' he asked,
nodding towards an alleyway.

She looked from him to the alley and then, with an
exasperated sigh, said, 'Jack is waiting for you.'

'To hell with Jack, I came here to see you.'

She ground her teeth. 'Well, nonetheless, Jack's up
there, cooling his heels, thinking he's got a meeting
with the great Salvador da Rocha, so you should go.'

'I'll go,' he agreed after a beat. 'If you'll give me
five minutes.'

She opened her mouth then closed it again and then,
with obvious consternation, yanked her wrist free and

rubbed it before cutting through the crowds towards the entrance to the alleyway. It was hardly the most romantic of settings—the ground was littered with cigarette butts, dull brick walls were covered with faded graffiti and there was the constant hum of passing strangers. But, whatever else had happened, since seeing Harper again everything Salvador had realised on the island had been confirmed.

And now it felt as though fighting for her, for them, was a matter of life and death. Not in the literal, mortal sense, but in the way that he would have no life if he didn't have Harper. He could exist, but that wasn't the same thing as living, as the last year had so clearly showed. It seemed as good a place as any to start.

'When you came to the island, you brought me back to life, Harper. I hadn't realised how shadowed my existence was, or why there was anything wrong with that, until you came and made me feel whole, more whole than I've ever been. You came and it was like a light had been turned on, a pervasive, beautiful light. And, when you left, the opposite happened: all the lights went out and I am anything but whole now. I miss you so much.'

Her face was impossible to read, but he knew enough to know his words weren't well received.

'Please don't do this,' she whispered, tortured.

'I know that what I said that last day was incredibly hurtful.'

She made a noise that might have been a withering laugh but it lacked all force.

'I didn't understand then how I felt…'

'Then let me enlighten you,' she said quietly, pulling

on her handbag again. 'You seem to like playing this sick little game with me—pushing me away, then pulling me back, pushing me away, pulling me back. That was you pushing me away. This is you trying to pull me back. But I'm not playing any more, Salvador. I'm not playing,' she repeated, the last words wobbly, tears falling from her eyes freely now. She dashed them away angrily and he could only stare. Her accusation was both fair and so damaging, because he hated himself then.

'I didn't want to feel this way about you.'

She tilted her face away, looking out of the alley towards the passing hoards.

'And you're right. But it wasn't a game, Harper. I have wanted you from the first moment I saw you, and loved you for almost as long. I wasn't pushing you away to torment you, but because I was fighting how I felt about you from the first day—only my feelings were so strong, I couldn't conquer them. I could make headway, sometimes, but not for long. You were here...' He pressed his fingers to his heart. 'You live here, in me, in my heart, and you always will.'

She jerked her face back to his, eyes frantic as they scanned his face. He thought for a moment he'd got through to her, but then her face paled and she shook her head.

'You're just raising the stakes now. The ultimate attempt to pull me back: you love me. But no one who's in love could say...could say...'

He groaned, hating himself for the words he'd spoken in his office that day.

'It was torture to say it,' he said. 'I was so angry at

myself for loving you when I hadn't been able to love her. I felt like every day with you was a betrayal, every feeling I had for you proof of my failure as a husband. None of that excuses my behaviour, but I just want to explain...'

She swallowed, then lifted her phone from her pocket. 'Jack will be waiting,' she said stiffly. He wasn't just losing her, he'd lost her. It was his worst nightmare come to fruition.

'To hell with Jack,' he said again.

'We had a deal.'

He cursed inwardly, because he was trying to win her back, and reneging on their compromise didn't seem like a good way to do that.

'I love you,' he said quietly, eyes boring into hers in the hope she could see the truth of what he was saying. 'I love you with every single fibre of who I am, with all of me. I'm done fighting it, done running from it. I want, for the rest of my life, to fight for us, to run to you, no matter where I am in this world. I am so in love with you, I cannot imagine a life without you in the centre of it. But if I have to, if you don't love me back, you will still always be the centre of who I am. Even if we're not together, I will love you. It's not a choice, Harper, it's who I am now.'

Another tear slid down her cheek. 'This isn't...it's not about if I love you or not,' she said unevenly. 'It's about whether I can be with you again.'

It was hardly anything—barely the cracking open of the door, a tiny ray of light in the midst of so much darkness—but it was *something*.

'It's about whether I can trust you.' She stared up at him. 'You're not the only one who's been hurt before, Salvador. It was *hard* for me to face how I felt about you and hard for me to come to you that morning and ask to stay.'

'I know, I know.' He couldn't help himself. He reached out, lifting his thumb and wiping away one of her tears, but then he kept his hand there, cocooned against the side of her face.

'And I stayed that whole day because it was my job but, in the back of my mind, I kept telling myself you'd come and apologise, that you'd come and see me, that you'd realise you'd reacted badly...'

'I wanted to. God, I wanted to.'

'But you didn't. And, every minute of that day, a part of me broke off and I don't know if you can ever put it back together. I just don't know. You let me go. You were just like my dad, just like Peter. You showed me that I don't have any value, just like they did.' She bit down on her lower lip and he ached for her, for the way she'd been treated and disrespected all her life.

'You are all that I value in this world,' he said angrily—the anger directed at himself. 'How can I show you that? How can I prove myself to you?'

She was silent, staring at him, lost and bereft. He lifted his free hand to her other cheek, holding her face, gently stroking with his thumbs.

'I love you,' he said, quietly. 'And I'm not going anywhere.'

'You live on an island,' she reminded him unevenly. 'Far, far away from here.'

'I want to live wherever you live,' he said with a lift of his shoulders.

'You can't move to Chicago.' She rolled her eyes.

'Why not?'

She stared at him in total confusion. 'I can't— I don't know if you're serious.'

'Harper, I love you. You *know* I love you. That last morning, when you suggested staying, it was because you understood how I felt, how you felt, and what we needed to do. I reacted terribly, and I will never forgive myself for that, but everything we shared before that, that was real. That's who we are.'

'But it's like I said—it's not about love, it's about choice. I did think you loved me,' she admitted carefully. 'But you chose not to be with me. What if you make that choice again? What if you decide in a week's time that, whether you love me or not, you can't be with me? I can't put the pieces of my life back together every time you decide that you're scared of what we feel for each other.'

'I was scared,' he admitted, and it was a lot for someone like Salvador to face that. He was generally fearless but not when it came to his heart. 'I was terrified of what would happen if I lost you too. Then I did lose you. Not to death, but to life and life choices, things that were completely in my control. I woke up every day and had to face how I felt and what I'd done and I know I could never do that again.

'I have no guarantees in life, Harper. I've seen what can happen, what can be taken from us without notice, or in the most awful ways, but only an absolute fool would pass up the happiness we share when we're together out of fear of what might happen. I don't know that we're going to get the great privilege of living together until we're old and grey, with a dozen grandkids scattered at our feet, but hell, I want to do everything I can to try. Don't you?' he pushed, tilting her face towards his. 'Look into your heart and tell me what you *want*.'

She closed her eyes, shielding herself from him, so he bit back a groan. He waited on tenterhooks, so terrified, knowing everything was riding on her answer.

She was silent so long, he thought he was burning up, and then she opened her eyes, frowning so she had a small divot between her brows.

'I want that,' she said finally, with a hint of surprise in her voice.

He wasn't sure he'd understood. 'You want…?'

'I want you. And me. Old and grey. Lots of grandkids and memories—good and bad, the kinds of memories you collect in a rich life that's well lived. I want to start living, Salvador, just like you said: when we're together, I'm alive. Most alive.' And then, sucking in a deep breath, she nodded slightly. 'I love you.'

They were the best words he'd ever heard. He pressed his forehead to hers, needing to fortify himself for what would come next. Because, when they kissed, it was as if all the pieces of heaven exploded and came back together inside them, all the matter in the universe existed just within them for the moment their lips meshed. To anyone walking past, it might have looked like just a couple sharing a passionate, secret embrace, but to Salvador and Harper it was a promise, as real and bonding as any marriage vows ever could be: they were both in this for real, for ever, because it was just exactly where they were meant to be.

On the twenty-ninth floor of the da Rocha Industries tower on Dearborn Street, Jack Wotton tapped his fingers against the dark wood of his desk, a frown on his face. It was not like da Rocha to be late. The man was renowned for his punctuality. He cast a glance at his watch again. Twenty past five. Where could he be?

Standing, he moved to the coffee machine right as his phone began to trill. He reached back for it, perching on the edge of his desk.

'Wotton? It's Salvador.' The man sounded…happy. Laughing… There was the sound of street noise in the background: people walking, cars, then the closing of a car door. 'Something's come up.' His voice sounded louder, because of the absence of street noise now. He was in his own car, Jack guessed.

'Not a problem, sir. Would you like to reschedule?'

There was a different sound, a little like clothing rustling. 'Yes. I'll call Monday.'

Jack pulled a face. 'Was there something specific you wanted to discuss?'

'Just a general touch-base.' Salvador's voice was muffled now, like his mouth was pressed against something. 'Everything's fine. Have a good weekend.'

Just before Jack disconnected the call, he thought he heard a woman's voice laughing and moaning at the same time. He shrugged his shoulders and abandoned the thought of a coffee, deciding instead to grab a beer on the way home. Everything was fine.

EPILOGUE

IN THE END, they chose sunset, the closing of the day, to mark the beginning of the rest of their lives, with a wedding on the edge of the island. The cove was behind them, water coming closer and closer with each minute that passed, with only a small handful of their dearest friends in attendance and Harper's mother listening online.

It was a perfect wedding, but that didn't matter to Harper. A wedding was just a moment, a single day out of a blanket of days that would form the rest of their lives. And not once, since having agreed to marry Salvador almost a year earlier, had she regretted her agreement for even one moment.

He was her other half in every way.

But he was more than that. He was the wind at her back, always pushing her to chase her own dreams, insisting on paying for her mother's medical care so that Harper could finally pursue her dreams of studying, which she did remotely. They lived on the island at first: Salvador had had a state-of-the-art medical facility built for Harper's mother, a place that had brought comfort to an old woman who smiled now, even when she didn't seem to know who or where she was.

Of course, it wasn't just the island, but soon there was the sound of grandchildren, little babies often brought by Harper to visit their nanny. The twins came first, two boys with their father's shock of dark hair and intelligent eyes. Then two daughters, born only eighteen months apart, and another daughter five years later, a miracle, surprise baby that neither had been expecting but both welcomed and loved with all their hearts.

Sofia was a part of their family, too. They spoke of Anna-Maria and her often, and took the children to the graves each year to mark their birthdays. It was important for them to understand that their family had begun with a different branch, a long time ago. And, though that branch had not survived, it didn't make it any less nor important to them all.

When Harper's mother passed, they were all sad, but also knew that she'd been set free. The grief of losing her mother was made more bearable because she had Salvador and their children to wrap her in their love, to hold her tight and listen to her stories of a time before the strokes, when her mother had been the be all and end all in Harper's life.

By the time the twins started school, they decided it was more practical to leave the island. They moved to New York then, so Harper could take up a position at a prestigious law firm. Within five years, she'd made partner, and two years after that senior partner. There had never been a prouder husband than Salvador.

They were blessed and they knew it—Salvador especially, after the losses he'd endured.

The da Rocha family travelled back to the island frequently for many, many years, so the place became a part of the fabric of their children's lives, and it was naturally where their oldest daughter chose to be married.

As the sun set on that momentous, beautiful day, and Salvador watched his wife with her silver hair and surrounded by their children—now adults—he couldn't help but smile and reflect on how close he'd come to wasting the precious gift that was his life. How close he'd come to letting Harper leave, because he'd been so scared that he might get hurt.

Instead, he'd been given a second chance, to live his life but also to honour the promises he'd made to his mother and Anna-Maria. Every single day of his life had been spent making the absolute most of that precious, second chance, and it always, always would be.

* * * * *

#4129 INNOCENT'S WEDDING DAY WITH THE ITALIAN
by Michelle Smart
Discovering that her billionaire fiancé, Enzo, will receive her inheritance if they wed, Rebecca leaves him at the altar and gives him twenty-four hours to explain himself. He vows his feelings are real, but dare Rebecca believe him and succumb to a passionate wedding night?

#4130 THE HOUSEKEEPER'S ONE-NIGHT BABY
by Sharon Kendrick
Letting someone close goes against Niccolò Macario's every instinct. When he receives news that shy housekeeper Lizzie Bailey, the woman he spent one scorching night with, is pregnant, Niccolò is floored—because his only thought is to find her and claim his child!

#4131 BACK TO CLAIM HIS CROWN
Innocent Royal Runaways
by Natalie Anderson
When Crown Prince Lucian returns from the dead to reclaim his throne, he stops his usurper's wedding, creating a media frenzy! He's honor-bound to provide jilted Princess Zara with shelter, and the chemistry between the ruthless royal and the virgin princess sparks an urgent, irresistible desire...

#4132 THE DESERT KING'S KIDNAPPED VIRGIN
Innocent Stolen Brides
by Caitlin Crews
When Hope Cartwright is kidnapped from her convenient wedding, she's sure she should feel outraged. But whisked away by Cyrus Ashkan, the sheikh she's been promised to from birth, Hope feels something *far* more dangerous—desire.

HPCNMRA0723

#4133 A SON HIDDEN FROM THE SICILIAN
by Lorraine Hall

Wary of billionaire Lorenzo Parisi's notorious reputation, Brianna Andersen vowed to protect her baby by keeping him a secret. Now the Sicilian knows the truth, and he's determined to be a father! As their blazing chemistry reignites, Brianna must admit the real risk may be to her heart...

#4134 HER FORBIDDEN AWAKENING IN GREECE
The Secret Twin Sisters
by Kim Lawrence

Nanny Rose Hill is surprised when irresistible CEO Zac Adamos personally proposes a job for her in Greece looking after his godson! She can't let herself get too close, but can the innocent really walk away without exploring the unforeseen passion Zac has awakened inside her?

#4135 THEIR DIAMOND RING RUSE
by Bella Mason

Self-made billionaire Julian Ford needs to secure funding from a group of traditional investors. His solution: an engagement to an heiress, and Lily Barnes-Shah fits the bill perfectly! Until their mutual chemistry makes Julian crave something outside the bounds of their temporary agreement...

#4136 HER CONVENIENT VOW TO THE BILLIONAIRE
by Jane Holland

When Sabrina Templeton returns to the orphanage from her childhood to stop her former sweetheart from tearing it down, playboy CEO Rafael Romano offers a shocking compromise... He'll hand it over if Sabrina becomes his convenient bride!

HPCNMRB0723

Get 3 FREE REWARDS!

We'll send you 2 FREE Books <u>plus</u> a FREE Mystery Gift.

Both the **Harlequin® Desire** and **Harlequin Presents®** series feature compelling novels filled with passion, sensuality and intriguing scandals.

HARLEQUIN
PLUS

Try the best multimedia
subscription service for romance
readers like you!

Read, Watch and Play.

Experience the easiest way to get
the romance content you crave.

Start your **FREE TRIAL** at
<u>www.harlequinplus.com/freetrial</u>.